THE
METAMORPHOSES
OF
METAPHOR

THE METAMORPHOSES OF METAPHOR

Essays in Poetry and Fiction

ALFRED CORN

Elisabeth Sifton Books
Viking

ELISABETH SIFTON BOOKS • VIKING
Viking Penguin Inc., 40 West 23rd Street, New York, New York 10010, U.S.A.
Penguin Books Ltd, Harmondsworth, Middlesex, England
Penguin Books Australia Ltd, Ringwood, Victoria, Australia
Penguin Books Canada Limited, 2801 John Street, Markham, Ontario, Canada L3R 1B4
Penguin Books (N.Z.) Ltd, 182–190 Wairau Road, Auckland 10, New Zealand

First published in 1987 by Viking Penguin Inc.
Published simultaneously in Canada

The author wishes to acknowledge periodicals in which earlier versions of these
essays first appeared:
The Georgia Review: "Elizabeth Bishop and John Hollander."
The Hudson Review: "Time to Read Proust." Used with permission. Copyright ©
1982 by The Hudson Review, Inc.
The Nation: "World of the Interior," previously published as two essays, "World of
the Interior" and "St. Peter's City."
Parnassus: "A Magma of Interiors," "The Anglo-Italian Relationship," and "Melan-
choly Pastorals." Used with permission.
Raritan: "Cavafy and Alexandrianism."
Shenandoah: "Elizabeth Bishop's Nativities."
Southwest Review: "Hart Crane's 'Atlantis.'"
The Yale Review: "Pilgrim in Metaphor," "Russian Encounters," "An Anglo-Irish
Novelist," and "Fishing by Obstinate Isles: Five Poets." Used with permission.
Copyright Yale University.
The essays on Stevens, Lowell, and Bishop were first given publicly during a
residency at George Mason University.
The essay on Crane was presented as part of a panel in Crane studies at the
N.E.M.L.A. convention in 1982.
"Pilgrim in Metaphor" was published as "Wallace Stevens and Poetic Ineffability"
in *Ineffability: Naming the Unnamable from Dante to Beckett*, edited by Peter S.
Hawkins and Anne Schotter, AMS Press, 1984.

LIBRARY OF CONGRESS CATALOGING IN PUBLICATION DATA
Corn, Alfred, 1943–
The metamorphoses of metaphor.
1. Literature, Modern—20th century—History and
criticism.   I. Title.
PN771.C64   1987   809'.04   86-40272
ISBN 0-670-81471-7

Printed in the United States of America
Set in Bembo
Designed by Beth Tondreau

To my teachers

If the imagination intoxicates the poet, it is not inactive in other men. The metamorphosis excites in the beholder an emotion of joy. The use of symbols has a certain power of emancipation and exhilaration for all men. We seem to be touched by a wand, which makes us dance and run about happily like children. We are like persons who come out of a cave or cellar into the open air. This is the effect on us of tropes, fables, oracles, and all poetic forms. Poets are thus liberating gods. Men have really got a new sense, and found within their world, another world, or nest of worlds; for, the metamorphosis once seen, we divine that it does not stop.

—Emerson, "The Poet"

Preface

I began publishing critical articles fifteen years ago, roughly at the same moment of my first serious efforts to write poetry. Although I had just left the Columbia University Graduate School (all work toward a doctorate in French literature completed except the dissertation), a keen interest in criticism and the literary tradition stayed with me; I have always been interested in criticism nearly as much as in imaginative writing in general. The two projects seem related: poets must discover critical faculties within themselves in order to test their first efforts at articulation, and critics, in order to write well about their subjects, must have at their disposal some of the gifts of poets, chiefly imagination and an availability to subtle, partly conscious responses.

As a reader, though, I like "pure" criticism (criticism for its own sake) no more than I like "pure" poetry. A good critic performs, but the performance is of no lasting interest unless it also informs. The point may be simply a question of time, of the expensiveness of time. Suppose I have just spent a year reading *A la recherche du temps perdu*, and I would now like to understand Proust's intentions better. Which critic will help me more, one whose main concern is to write a "prose poem" about the novel, or one who has spent weeks and months, perhaps years, in following up references and discovering patterns of meaning not easily grasped on one reading? Of course I hope the informative critic has writerly abilities compatible with the authors examined—a readable and interesting style, values something more than conventional, and, as I said before, imagination and intuition. But the first thing I ask of a critical work is that it tell me something—factual, thematic, formal—that I did not know beforehand. Without the critic's help, I have little chance to reach anything more than a conversational knowledge of the always-increasing body of significant literary works, or to look at the enterprise of literary art from fresh perspectives.

Some readers were shocked by Vladimir Nabokov's critical writings when they were published after his death. Here was one of the most raffiné artists of the twentieth century suddenly revealed as passionately concerned about the precise cut of certain Restoration overcoats, or domestic architecture in Prague, *because* this arcane knowledge would improve our reading of *Eugene Onegin* and *The Metamorphosis*. But of course it is precisely Nabokov's civilized acerbity that accounts for his willingness to take up the task of patient factual explanation. Because he was one of the least modest novelists, he could be one of the most altruistic critics, content to supply necessary information from his immense store, all in the interest of the authors themselves, who would have only the detachment of the *outre tombe* to help them bear the misunderstandings occasioned by their work. Nabokov the novelist was only laboring in behalf of his guild, whose members were often at the mercy of superficial criticism. Someone had to set the example. Meanwhile, the place for lofty imaginative exploits and intricate verbal invention was in his fiction.

All the chapters in this book were written (in their first versions) on assignment, but they represent only about half of the critical writing I have published. I have included here only those pieces that seemed to say something apart from the immediate task of evaluation; in one or two cases I have revised what was nominally a review into an essay. This volume is obviously an assemblage and was not conceived as a single book, but I believe it has roughly the same kind of unity found in a collection of short stories. A single temperament is at work in all the essays, and, though the style varies according to the occasion, still I seem to recognize it always as mine. Beyond that, I have persistently returned to certain preoccupations throughout the volume: I am interested in the relationship of individual authors to a tradition or to several traditions.

In particular, two traditions come back over and again for discussion. One is the long line of the Dantean legacy, central for English and American poetry since the Romantic period; the other is the Symbolist movement in all its transformations, which continue even into the present. Arthur Symons introduced French Symbolism to the English public, and his introduction was taken a step further in America by Edmund Wilson (*Axel's Castle*). Randall Jarrell (in "The End of the Line") showed how American modernism was a late variant of Symbolism, but his essay was published in book form only recently, long after his death. I know of no study that follows that tradition directly into the present—or, for that matter, one that traces the origins of Symbolism to its sources. If Baudelaire is the founder of Symbolism, that is only to say that he developed it by adapting his form of fallen Christianity to the theories of E. T. A. Hoffmann concerning sense perception, and to the visionary inwardness of Emerson. It is clear that Baudelaire had read the first "Nature" essay before writing his sonnet "Correspondances," and of course this sonnet became the first *manifeste du Symbolisme*. Poe was an important figure to the fin de siècle, but so was Whitman, and by the time of Apollinaire, Whitman had come to the fore as the prophet of a new age. The Americanness of the French tradition since Baudelaire perhaps explains why Symbolism entered so readily into the mainstream of American poetry.

The cultural prestige of France in Europe plus the fact that Emerson was read as widely as French authors help account for the influence of Symbolism in other countries as well. In this collection, I discuss some Russian instances of that influence (Pasternak and Bely) and one Italian instance (Montale). As for the Americans I have written about here, I hope that these essays will make it seem natural to find, for example, Baudelaire's "Correspondances" sonnet alluded to in Elizabeth Bishop's "The Bight," or a Mallarméan concern for the supreme and final Book in Stevens. Some observers might remark that Symbolism continues into contemporary writing only as a faint echo nearly drowned out by journalistic fact; but to say as much is to forget that the American tradition since its Puritan foundations has always treated fact allegorically.

Is it mere coincidence that Dante arises so often in these same discussions? Perhaps not. He and Shakespeare were the preferred modern authors of the Romantics, and when we consider his vast undertaking, a vision at once autobiographical, aesthetic, and theological, we see that all of the Symbolist preoccupations are prefigured in it—with the single difference that Dante drew on an orthodoxy for which the Symbolists could feel nostalgia but nothing more. The loss of belief was experienced in literature as the loss of Dante, an event that was both a bereavement and a liberation. It was no longer plausible or desirable to attempt anything on the scale of his vision. Only after the face of Christianity changed and its theology was brought closer in harmony with post-Enlightenment knowledge could writers like Montale and Eliot take it up again and bring it into literature, once more under the sign of Dante—a Dante less like a father than like a son, and, apparently, one who had read the Symbolists.

The title for this book may need accounting for. When Ovid in his epilogue to *Metamorphoses* invokes the immortality and unchangeability of art to preserve his book, he touches on a central paradox. The subject matter of art is fluctuant reality, out of which something immobile and permanent is forged. "Ever-shifting Proteus," in Ovid's poem, tells the Trojan hero Peleus how to conquer a fellow seadweller, the nymph Thetis: the hero must bind her with a net so that she will no longer be able to elude his embraces by changing form. To allegorize the myth for poetry, we may say that form (in its widest sense) is just that net, a container for all the changing aspects of reality the author strives to bring into the immutable realm of art. Yet the artist must be faithful to a mutable world, even as it is being transformed into art. Hence the universal reliance on metaphor—a trope, a lens, an arm of epistemology—which keeps some of the fluctuant quality of life itself, relocating the shimmering indeterminacy of reality in the mind of the reader. For metaphors can never be entirely rationalized; they continue to generate the energies of meaning as long as they are interrogated. To comment on metaphors in a work of art is an act of divination or, at least, like reading a Rorschach inkblot. Indelible and fixed themselves in a literary text, they induce nonfixity in the "text" of the reader. Metaphors metamorphose under our very eyes. They may serve to shed the light of meaning on some small homely object, as when Elizabeth Bishop compares the herring scales stuck to an old fisherman's shirt to sequins; or suggest an overarching structural analogy, as when Proust makes us see his long novel as a cathedral, one that is also sailing down the river of Time like the ark or the ship of Faith. Finally, it is also possible to speak of artists whose entire career is a metaphor for some interior quest, the slow revelation of a spiritual truth. The first essay proposes as much for the case of Wallace Stevens—and without further preamble I leave you at its door.

Contents

I
PILGRIMS
IN
METAPHOR

I

Pilgrim in Metaphor: Wallace Stevens

Wittgenstein enjoins us not to speak of those things that do not belong to discourse: "Whereof we cannot speak, we must remain silent." And yet wonderfully often speakers or writers manage to find ways of talking approximately or indirectly about experience that they actually hold to be outside or above the reach of words. Ways of overcoming the obstacles to speech vary; they are part of the set of stylistic and contextual qualities that confer identity and identifiability on a writer. Of course the unsayable or "ineffable" itself is not the same category for all potential speakers (few of whom, in any case, will be writers). In certain religious faiths, it is accounted a sin to make any mention of the name of God, or of the divine; thereof, the righteous will keep silent. In other instances, both religious and secular, verbal expression is not held to be sinful or contaminating but merely inadequate and paltry, compared to some areas of private experience. This group includes most of the writers thought of as being concerned with the ineffable. It includes, for example, the later Wallace Stevens; but the early Stevens is often best understood as belonging to yet another contingent. This third group includes the temperaments who find imaginative writing (in a nontrivial sense) impossible, because they see no transcendent sanctions that could be drawn on to form truthful statements in literature. For them, the universe is silent, and thus silence is truer than any utterance. To invent is to fabricate, to fabricate is base or invalid, and so there is truly nothing to write.

It is tempting to call this last obstacle to speech "negative ineffability"; and it is one that determines much of Stevens's early poetry. The negative mythological figure for the world of *Harmonium* is the Snow Man, who perceives "Nothing that is not there, and the nothing that is." If there had been no other figures in the pantheon Stevens invented for his poetry, he could not have written many more poems. But Stevens began to imagine other altars, engaging in an extended poetic pilgrimage and entertaining many ideas on the nature of truth, of the imagination, and of the philosophical status of poetic utterance. Why Stevens didn't from the start understand poems as "fictions," and statements in them as hypothetical, has to do both with his own skeptic's temperament (which must have been useful in his bond surety investigations for the Hartford Accident and Indemnity Company) and with modernist developments in American poetry during the first two decades of this century (which cannot be taken up here in detail). In any case, the notion that the poet "nothing affirmeth and therefore never lieth" clearly failed to satisfy Stevens: poems must be true, otherwise they are of no importance.

Poems must be true because, with the death of God, the arts must come to replace religion. In a letter to Barbara Church (which is dated August 12, 1947, but reflects beliefs he developed during his student days at Harvard fifty years earlier) Stevens said. "As scepticism becomes both complete and profound, we face either a true civilization or a blank; and literature ought to be one of the factors to determine the choice. Certainly, if civilization is to consist only of man himself, and it is, the arts must take the place of divinity, at least as a stage in whatever general principle or progress is involved." What did living in a universe empty of deity mean for Stevens? The blankness, cold, and misery mentioned in "The Snow Man" are metaphoric ways of conveying it, and a more succinct formulation is found in his *Adagia*: "Reality is a vacuum." Against human mortality, suffering, and meaninglessness, Stevens proposes the imagination as a redemptive force, to push back (here he inverts the metaphor) against the "pressure of reality." The imagination is also the psychological faculty that allows poems to be written; indeed, the proportional equation "silence is to speech as death is to life" stands at the center of Stevens's poetic vocation. If one can write poems, one may find a sanction for human existence, and so may live.

Stevens's view of the "imagination as value," a conviction he repeats in many prose contexts and draws on as the emotional substance for so many poems, could be seen as absolute, no less comprehensive than a belief in the divine. Just as frequently, however, he expressed an opposing view: "The ultimate value is reality." When poetry fails to reflect reality, it presents merely a "dead romantic," a "falsification." Stevens is never clear and precise as to how the false imagination is to be distinguished from the true, the dead romanticism from the live; but, in general, he seems to look for a marriage, a mystic union between the imagination and reality, without explaining how wedlock is to be effected. (Readers will recall, in this connection, the fable of the "mystic marriage" between the captain and the maiden Bawda in *Notes Toward a Supreme Fiction.)*

It is apparent that, although Stevens was drawn to philosophical issues and discourse, he did not demand of himself the development of a system organized and expressed with philosophical rigor: "What you don't allow for," he said, "is the fact that one moves in many directions at once. No man of imagination is prim: the thing is a contradiction in terms." This is as much a program as a description: Stevens wishes to *postpone* the hasty formulation of a system, to forestall final conclusions. He wishes to rest neither in the imagination nor in reality because rest is undesirable; is hard to distinguish from philosophical or psychological stasis or perhaps paralysis; and life is supremely a question of movement and change. In a letter to Sister Bernetta Quinn of April 7, 1948, he says: "However, I don't want to turn to stone under your very eyes by saying 'This is the centre that I seek and this alone.' Your mind is too much like my own for it to seem to be an evasion on my part to say merely that I do seek a centre and expect to go on seeking it. I don't say that I do not expect to find it. It is the great necessity even without specific identification."

Even if philosophical or religious finality were attainable, Stevens recognizes that the "never-resting mind" would not accept any such finality: "Again, it would be the merest improvisation to say of any image of the world, even though it was an image with which a vast accumulation of imaginations had been content, that it was the chief image. The imagination itself would not remain content with it nor allow us to do so. It is the irrepressible revolutionist." The view of truth (and life) that emerges from these statements is one shared by many modern philosophers of mind: truth is not a set of propositions but is a psychological process. For Stevens, there is (and should be) a constant oscillation between the categories reason/fact and imagination/fable. A poetry or a life content with either of these opposing terms will not constitute fulfillment. Poets (considered exemplary for all of us) will always be seeking, voyaging, and questing, so long as they are alive.

This summary of philosophic and poetic ideas, though it is partial and perhaps supererogatory for the Stevens scholar, may retrace for nonspecialists the steps taken during Stevens's long career. In early Stevens, the ground is, generally, bare reality, the wintry landscape of nothingness seen by the Snow Man; the *figure* is the imagination that comes to free the mind from its subjection to reality. In the later Stevens it is more often the imagination that is the ground, all-pervasive and easily available. Reality then comes to seem the figure brought in as a contrast, a "refreshment," a cleansing away of the dull fictional film habitually covering our view of things. The emblematic figure typically summoned by Stevens in 1922 is the "One of Fictive Music"; for the later Stevens, it is the "Necessary Angel" of reality. But, more and more often, Stevens begins to call for a fusion of reality and imagination into one entity, variously referred to as the Grand Poem, the Supreme Fiction, the Central Mind, or the Central Imagination. This hypothetical category comes to seem in some sense possible to Stevens, even though it always remains a projection. There is a constant future-tenseness to Stevens's visionary insight; he gives notes *toward* the Supreme Fiction, *prologues* "to what is possible." A title Stevens considered for his first book was *The Grand Poem: Preliminary Minutiae;* and the early Stevens could say, "The book of moonlight is not written yet nor half begun," and, "Music is not yet written but is to be."

The implication is that Stevens believes the great book can be written and that he will do it. By 1943 and the writing of *Notes,* it is apparent that the projective character of his vision has crystallized as doctrine. In an essay composed that same year he says, "The incredible is not a part of poetic truth. On the contrary, what concerns us in poetry, as in everything else, is the belief of credible people in credible things. It follows that poetic truth is the truth of credible things, not so much that it is actually so, as that it might be so." A few years later, in *The Auroras of Autumn,* he would put the matter this way:

> There is or may be a time of innocence
> As pure principle. Its nature is its end,
> That it should be, and yet not be. . . .

Although Stevens's summum bonum belongs to futurity, his adumbrations of it remind one of other poets' efforts to recount mystic experiences actually undergone, remembered wordlessly, and termed ineffable in the usual sense. Here it will be useful to consider some of Stevens's reflections on ultimate value, which, in this instance, he terms "nobility":

I mean that nobility which is our spiritual height and depth; and while I know how difficult it is to express it, nevertheless I am bound to give a sense of it. Nothing could be more evasive and inaccessible. Nothing distorts itself and seeks disguise more quickly. There is a shame of disclosing it and in its definite presentations, a horror of it. But there it is. The fact that it is there is what makes it possible to invite to the reading and writing of poetry men of intelligence and desire for life. I am not thinking of the ethical or the sonorous or at all of the manner of it. The manner of it is, in fact, its difficulty, which each man must feel each day differently for himself. I am not thinking of the solemn, the portentous or demoded. On the other hand, I am evading a definition. If it is defined, it will be fixed and it must not be fixed. As in the case of an external thing, nobility resolves itself into an enormous number of vibrations, movements, changes. To fix it is to put an end to it. ["The Noble Rider and the Sound of Words," in *The Necessary Angel*]

"Vibrations, movements, changes"; much of Stevens's poetic style is covered by these terms, and they constitute part of the difficulty of his "manner." The whole passage, with its strenuous effort to get at the inexpressible, suggests that Stevens's first intuitions concerning the nature of a supreme and always future fiction may have come to him out of his struggle with style and expression itself. The title of the essay from which this passage is drawn refers not only to nobility, but also to "the sound of words." Consider then another passage from the same essay in *The Necessary Angel*, one where Stevens discusses our feeling for words themselves.

The deepening need for words to express our thoughts and feelings which, we are sure, are all the truth that we shall ever experience, having no illusions, makes us listen to words when we hear them, loving them and feeling them, makes us search the sound of them, for a finality, a perfection, an unalterable vibration, which it is only within the power of the acutest poet to give them.

A paradox present in this apologia for words and their sounds, words at their most *physical,* in short, is that the principal result is immaterial and nonverbal. Stevens says as much in another essay ("Effects of Analogy"): "There is always an analogy between nature and the imagination, and possibly poetry is merely the strange rhetoric of that parallel: a rhetoric in which the feeling of one man is communicated to another in words of the exquisite appositeness that takes away all their verbality."

The inference, then, is that our surest clue, our only available insight, into the nature of the "central imagination" are words and their sound. Unlike most poets of mystic insight, Stevens does not deplore the inadequacies of his medium; he celebrates it and becomes its hierophant. Is it appropriate to call this a "verbal sublime"? There is at least one major precedent for it in literature—the poetry of Mallarmé. Other affinities between the two poets have been noted: the view of the poet as a sacramental figure; the recourse to music as the best analogy for poetry; and the belief (Mallarmé's belief) in a final Book that the world was meant to become, a Book not yet written. (This must be one of the sources of Stevens's Supreme Fiction.) In actual fact, the French poet Stevens most often mentions is not Mallarmé, but Paul Valéry, who, however, belongs to the same tradition: Stevens wrote prefaces for two of Valéry's dialogues, *Eupalinos* and *Dance and the Soul,* when these were translated and published in the Bollingen series.

The view of the sacramental role of the poet, whose poems may be considered incantations or prayers, is not foreign to Valéry's own poetics and fits well with something he once said about prayer and unknown tongues (his prototype, obviously, was Roman Catholic liturgical Latin): "C'est pourquoi il ne faut prier qu'en paroles inconnues. Rendez l'énigme à l'énigme, énigme pour énigme. Elevez ce qui est mystère en vous à ce qui est mystère en soi. Il y a en vous quelque chose d'égal à ce qui vous passe" ("That is why one should pray only in unknown words. Return the enigma to the enigma, enigma for enigma. Lift up what is mystery in you to what is mystery in itself. There is in you something equal to what goes beyond you" ["Comme le Temps est calme," translation mine]). For his part, Stevens said (in the *Adagia),* "Poetry is a search for the inexplicable," and "It is necessary to propose an enigma to the mind." Although he did not write his poems in Latin, no small number of the incantations Stevens proposed to his mind (and ours) employ French words; and much of his vocabulary (in the poems) is composed of archaism, coinages, and sound-words either onomatopoetic in nature, or modeled on Elizabethan singing syllables ("hey-derry-derry-down," etc.), or similar to scat-singing in jazz ("shoo-shoo-shoo," and "ric-a-nic," for example). The point is, no doubt, to invent that "imagination's Latin" Stevens speaks of in *Notes Toward a Supreme Fiction.* It is in this sense, perhaps, that he wished to be understood when he said, "Personally, I like words to sound wrong." An overstatement; but it is certainly true that Stevens has one of the most noticeable styles in our poetry; and it could be said that he wrote an English that often sounds as if it were another language. How is the poet to overcome universal silence? One way is to make a joyful noise.

In view of his high claims for poetry, it appears that nothing can be more serious than poetic style. In his essay "Two or Three Ideas," he proposes that, as poems and their style are one, so men and their style are one; the same may be said of "the gods." Then why not interchange *all* the terms? The style of men, and their poems, and their gods, are one; thus, style is an index of the divine. The task, as Stevens saw it, was to discover and compose a style that would serve as just such an index. Already noted is Stevens's reliance on a special diction to give the effect of "otherness," of enigmatic mystery, an effect appropriate to a supreme, future fulfillment. Beyond that, the poet must include in his repertoire accents of grandeur and nobility. Stevens draws on several sources for these. Anyone who has heard him read, or has heard recordings of his reading, will have immediately noted the resemblance of his elocutionary style to that of the Protestant minister—the intonations of prayer, the accents of exhortation. By the same token, the language of Stevens's poems is often Christian in flavor: "Sister and mother, and diviner love. . . ."; "Whose spirit is this? we said, because we knew / It was the spirit that we sought and knew / That we should ask this often as she sang." Stevens is like other Romantic poets in adapting Christian rhetoric to his purposes, and, of course, he borrows directly from Wordsworth, Shelley, Keats, and Whitman themselves. More surprising, however, is his enormous reliance on Shakespeare, and not merely for personae like Peter Quince and Marina. He tends to draw on Shakespeare's high rhetoric for certain moments of large, visionary utterance. When, in "Final Soliloquy of the Interior Paramour," he writes, "We say God and the imagination are one . . . / How high that highest candle lights the dark," it is impossible not to think of Portia's lines in Act V of *The Merchant of Venice:* "How far that little candle throws his beams! / So shines a good deed in a naughty world." Stevens's recasting is no disgrace to its source; and part of the power of these lines lies in the connection the reader makes between the sense of Shakespeare's greatness and the philosophical amplitude of the issues being treated in this poem.

Stevens has come so far from "the nothing that is" as to speak of deity, God, with a capital letter.* The gradual pil-

---

*The question of the precise nature of Stevens's religious beliefs is an interesting one. To be taken into account are statements made at different times in his life, statements as various as: "Proposita: 1. God and the imagination are one. 2. The thing imagined is the imaginer. . . . Hence, I suppose, the imaginer is God" *(Adagia,* p. 178). "It is the belief and not the god that counts" *(Adagia,* p. 171). "God is in me or else is not at all (does not exist)" *(Adagia,* p. 172). "I am not an atheist although I do not believe today in the same God in whom I believed when I was a boy" (letter to Sister Bernetta Quinn, December 21, 1951). "At my age it would be nice to be able to read more and be myself more and to make up my mind about God, say, before it is too late, or at least before he makes up his mind about me" (letter to Thomas McGreevy, October 24, 1952). Finally, according to an account given to Peter Brazeau (in *Parts of a World: Wallace Stevens Remembered*) by

grimage from Nothing to Something recapitulated in his career as a poet is a process enacted constantly (though on a
much smaller scale) in his later poems. The typical embodiment of the change is metaphor, which he describes variously
as "metamorphosis," "transformation," "transmutation,"
and even "apotheosis." Metaphor is the agency by which a
real but empty thing is imaginatively transformed into something "unreal" and fulfilling. The poem as a whole is to be
taken as an extended metaphor. Two passages from Stevens's
essays in *The Necessary Angel* point to this process:

> The way a poet feels when he is writing, or after he has writ-
> ten, a poem that completely accomplishes his purpose is evi-
> dence of the personal nature of his activity. To describe it by
> exaggerating it, he shares the transformation, not to say
> apotheosis, accomplished by the poem. It must be this experi-
> ence that makes him think of poetry as possibly a phase of
> metaphysics; and it must be this experience that teases him
> with that sense of the possibility of a remote, a mystical *vis* or
> *noeud vital* to which reference has already been made.

> Certainly a sense of the infinity of the world is a sense of
> something cosmic. It is cosmic poetry because it makes us
> realize that we are creatures, not of a part, which is our every-
> day limitation, but of a whole for which, for the most part,
> we have as yet no language. This sudden change of a lesser life
> for a greater one is like a change of winter for spring or any
> other transmutation of poetry.

The metaphor of the passage from winter to spring as representing the shift from one ontology to another is very frequent in Stevens, and, in fact, is the basis for the final poem
in the 1954 edition of his *Collected Poems,* "Not Ideas about
the Thing but the Thing Itself." Recalling that "metaphor,"

---

the Reverend Arthur Hanley, chaplain at Saint Francis hospital in 1955,
Stevens underwent an eleventh-hour conversion to Roman Catholicism a
few days before his death.

by its etymology, can suggest the notion of "transport" (itself a term with several possible meanings), one is given a clue to part of the intention in a volume like *Transport to Summer* (1947), which may be understood as a book-length embodiment of the central doctrine of metaphysical transformation. The volume opens with a summer poem, "God is Good. It Is a Beautiful Night" (to be read, "God = Good = Summer Night"), but, not resting with that, goes on to include poems oscillating back and forth between summer and winter settings, and ends with *Notes*, which includes the same constant pendulum swing, beginning with autumn and ending with the "Fat girl, terrestrial, my summer, my night." If it is desirable to isolate a central controlling "structure" in the Stevensian imagination, no doubt it is the idea of metaphoric transformation that must be proposed. At the lower end of the scale, this provides the endless variety of tropes invented by Stevens in the poems; at the next level, it presents the poem under the aspect of transfiguration or apotheosis; and then, the *volume* of poems as a change from the wintry mind to the summum bonum of summer. It is fair to say, too, that Stevens's long poetic career moves generally from a predominantly wintry metaphysics to a more positive and reassuring stance. And, if seasonal change is the most frequent *temporal* metaphor for revelation in Stevens, the most frequent *spatial* one is "Pilgrimage":

> The number of ways of passing between the traditional two fixed points of a man's life, that is to say, of passing from the self to God, is fixed only by the limitations of space, which is limitless. The eternal philosopher is the eternal pilgrim on that road.

The metaphorical transformation of reality, then, was actually a kind of religious pilgrimage for Stevens. And its completion he viewed as an apotheosis, but one that must be undertaken again and again—it is never final. The exact nature of deity is not to be stated; Stevens is content with formulae such as the "central imagination" or the "central poem." The act of writing offers the only clue Stevens has to the nature of the divine, and the intuitions of poetry all have to do with a directional transformation, from thing to figure, from fact to fable. A poem such as "A Primitive Like an Orb," which touches on all these ideas, can be read almost as a catechism for Stevens's beliefs about poetry and its relationship to the divine. This meditation on "The essential poem at the centre of things" is a fine sample, too, of Stevensian rhetoric at its most expansive and harmonious, a rhetoric developed from Christian, idealist-philosophical, and Shakespearean language. Three stanzas from the poem:

> II
> We do not prove the existence of the poem.
> It is something seen and known in lesser poems.
> It is the huge, high harmony that sounds
> A little and a little, suddenly,
> By means of a separate sense. It is and it
> Is not and, therefore, is. In the instant of speech,
> The breadth of an accelerando moves,
> Captives the being, widens—and was there. . . .
>
> IV
> One poem proves another and the whole,
> For the clairvoyant men that need no proof:
> The lover, the believer and the poet.
> Their words are chosen out of their desire,
> The joy of language, when it is themselves.
> With these they celebrate the central poem,
> The fulfillment of fulfillments, in opulent,
> Last terms, the largest, bulging still with more,
>
> V
> Until the used-to earth and sky, and the tree
> And cloud, the used-to tree and used-to cloud,
> Lose the old uses that they made of them,
> And they: these men, and earth and sky, inform
> Each other by sharp informations, sharp,

Free knowledges, secreted until then,
Breaches of that which held them fast. It is
As if the central poem became the world . . .

The central poem of the world is clearly not, here, a nothingness. The universal vacancy so apparent to Stevens in the
first phase of his career has come to be replaced by a sense and
a rhetoric of fullness. A primary source of his conviction as to
the certitude of that fullness is the feeling emanating from
that very rhetoric, in poems lesser than the "essential poem."
The obstacle to utterance is removed, for Stevens, by the
transforming power and cosmic harmony manifest in *poesis*
itself.

2

A Magma of Interiors: John Ashbery's *Self-Portrait in a Convex Mirror*

"To create a work of art that the critic cannot even talk about ought to be the artist's chief concern," John Ashbery once said *(Art News,* May 1972). This statement was made about painters, but there's every chance Ashbery would appropriate the same concern for poetry as well. He said, in another review, "Poets when they write about artists always tend to write about themselves." The ambition to outdistance criticism can arise simply as a human dislike of being pinned down—"Is that all there is?"—but more often indicates a commitment to innovation and evolution in art. A recurrent problem in the evolution of twentieth-century art is that so many writers, not content with being *absolument moderne,* have then supposed they ought to be futuristic; and what is more poignant than yesterday's imagination of the future? In practice, the will to innovation often produces works nobody can talk about, yes, but more to the point, works that nobody *cares* to talk about.

This does not apply to John Ashbery. His originality is, unmistakably, the kind that comes as a by-product of sincerity. One feels that Ashbery would consider it somehow "false" to write with any greater reliance on conventions of communication as they already exist—even if those conventions included some established by the early work of John Ashbery.

All of Ashbery's books have been difficult to talk about, and *Self-Portrait in a Convex Mirror* resists analysis and evaluation as valiantly as the others. Still, the merit of his work now seems to be evident to nearly everybody, at least, the work beginning with *The Double Dream of Spring,* including *Three Poems,* and culminating with the poems collected in *Self-Portrait.* In this climate of admiration and critical hesitation it's possible to conclude that some kind of corner has been turned in the movement—I don't say progress—of literature. Although Richard Howard, Harold Bloom, and David Kalstone have broken important ground in Ashbery criticism, at present, and of necessity, it remains largely a project.

It's tempting to fall back on the methods of apophatic or "negative" theology and list everything the poems in this volume are *not,* but I think I'll plunge right in and say what they are, at least how most of them function for one reader. The poems seem to be imitations of consciousness, "meditations" about the present, including the moment of writing. Their ambition is to render as much of psychic life as will go onto the page—perceptions, emotions, and concepts, memory and daydream, thought in all of its random and contradictory character, patterned according to the "wave interference" produced by all the constituting elements of mind—a "magma of interiors," one of the poems puts it.

Ashbery's method is allusive, associative, and disjunctive, rather than logical, dramatic, or narrative. A typical extended poem will launch itself, or maybe wake up to find itself already in transit, throw out a fertile suggestion, make connections, go into reverse, change key, short-circuit, suffer enlightenment, laugh, nearly go over the edge, regard itself with disbelief, irony, and pathos, then sign off with an inconclusive gesture. The texture of many of the poems reminds me of Gaudí's mosaics in the Barcelona Parque Güell, where broken-up fragments of colored tile with all kinds of figuration—Moorish-geometrical, floral, pictorial—are carefully reassembled in a new and arresting whole:

Nathan the Wise is a good title it's a reintroduction
Of heavy seeds attached by toggle switch to long loops leading
Out of literature and life into worldly chaos in which
We struggle two souls out of work for it's a long way back to
The summation meanwhile we live in it "gradually getting used
    to"
Everything and this overrides living and is superimposed on it
As when a wounded jackal is tied to a waterhole the lion does
    come

["Lithuanian Dance Band"]

It's possible of course to consider this kind of pied beauty not simply an "imitation of consciousness" but rather a new synthetic kind of experience too underdetermined or maybe overdetermined to render consciousness accurately, and so existing on a purely contemplative, aesthetic plane. Obviously, these two efforts overlap and blend: "imitation" in art is never duplication, and it always involves some synthesis; but nothing lifelike can be synthesized in art unless it can seem to belong to consciousness. In the measure, then, that an imitation becomes more stylized and synthetic, its resemblance to anyone's consciousness proportionately decreases—it becomes more purely artful. I don't see the poems in Self-Portrait as all occupying a fixed point on the spectrum that moves from direct representation of a stream of consciousness to a purely composed and synthetic experience. Nor would I assume that any of the poems were pure products of "automatic writing." If there's an automatic writer that can rap out phrases like the following, one wants the thing installed immediately:

. . . This was one of those night rainbows
In negative color. As we advance, it retreats; we see

We are now far into a cave, must be. Yet there seem to be
Trees all around, and a wind lifts their leaves, slightly.
                                    ["Märchenbilder"]

In a sense, all good writing is an "imitation of consciousness" insofar as that is compatible with the selectivity
required for effective, beautiful communication. A special
quality of consciousness as imitated by Ashbery, however, is
its inclusiveness, or, more precisely, its magnification: into
these poems come minute or translucent mental events that
would escape a less acute gaze, an attention less rapt. It's the
same degree of magnification, I think, used to apprehend the
tropismes in Nathalie Sarraute's early fiction, though Ashbery
lacks the fury and venom characteristic of her work. In this
poetry, the unconscious—that misnomer—is in agreeable
tension with the conceptual, composing mind; the free inter-
weaving of the known and the about-to-be-known makes for
a rich experiential texture in which guesswork, risk, and discovery contribute almost a tactile quality to the overall
patterning.

Imitating consciousness, or the stream of consciousness, as
a writing method is sown with thistles for any writer without
genius or at least without a mental complexion as special and
original as John Ashbery's. Zany, elegiac, informed—and
sometimes interestingly deformed—by an acquaintance with
arcane or demotic or technological subject matter, it's a sensibility one thread of which has been described by the narrator
of *A Season in Hell:*

> I liked idiotic paintings, carvings over doorframes, vaudeville
> drop-scenes, sign-boards, dimestore prints, antiquated liter-
> ature, church Latin, pornographic books with bad spelling,
> novels by our grandmothers, fairy tales, children's books, old
> operas, silly lyrics, uncouth meters.

Cultural allusion in Ashbery goes high as well as low—
classic and sometimes obscure works of music, painting, and

literature come into mention, without, however, being presented as "letters of credit," as they sometimes are with inse-
cure writers; so that it would be wrong to call Ashbery's
poetry "literary." The charge more often than not is made
disingenuously, by the way. No subject matter is safely out
of poetry's reach, even literary subject matter. It strikes me as
unnatural, even artificial, to proscribe literary or cultural allusion from poetry in the age of the paperback, the LP, and
color reproduction. If recondite allusion is a fault, then it
ought to be acknowledged that, at present, readers of poetry
are more likely to have accurate perceptions and definite feelings about, say, the *Pastoral* Symphony, or *The Cherry Or-
chard,* or *The Twittering Machine,* than about the Snake River,
the hornbeam tree, or the engine of a Diamond Reo. It's true
that art can come to conceal the world around us and act as a
filter to unmediated experience (not necessarily a bad thing—
who would *always* take experience unmediated?) so that too
many people get described as looking like "Bronzinos," and
too often office routines are summed up as "Kafkaesque";
but Ashbery avoids triteness—or any sort of creative abdica-
tion. I'd say the cultural allusions were brought in simply as
part of an environment, the nuts and bolts of daily life in a
cultural capital.

Most of the allusions in this volume seem to have to do
with music; in fact, many of the poems have musical titles:
"Grand Galop" (Liszt), "Tenth Symphony" (Mahler's unfinished one?), "Märchenbilder" (the Schumann Opus 113),
and "Scheherazade," which could be Rimsky-Korsakov or
possibly Ravel, if we allow for English spelling. The texts of
the poems include many other musical allusions; and, in a
published interview, Ashbery has stated that he often writes
with music playing, as a stimulant. All of this ought to be a
tip-off. The Symbolist (and Paterian) doctrine that all the arts
aspire to the condition of music has been, implicitly, a point
of departure for development of modernist art in this century
and stands behind the two distinctive tendencies in that art—

the drive toward abstraction and the absolute fusion of form and content.

Ashbery is something of an American Symbolist, and his poem "The Tomb of Stuart Merrill" is by way of an *hommage* to a not too well known American poet of the fin de siècle who expatriated, wrote in French, and enlisted in the Symbolist movement. (Incidentally, if mention of the French tradition always comes up in any discussion of Ashbery, nonetheless his Americanness remains obvious and inescapable, as Wallace Stevens's does. Ashbery only occasionally reproduces the formal restraint, sensuousness, and lucidity of characteristically French art; more often his work exhibits the sincerity, distrust of artifice, and studied awkwardness we associate with achievement in the American grain.)

Valéry, a good Symbolist and word-musician, said that content in art was only impure form, and Ashbery's poem "Soonest Mended" suggested that meaning might be "cast aside some day / When it had been outgrown." Of course meaning is never outgrown until life is; nor can meaning ever be cast aside, really, because the act of doing so then becomes the "meaning" of a text. No, John Ashbery's poetry does retain content, a content, however, radically fused with form—the result is that paraphrases of the poems are more than usually lame, if not downright impossible.

The poems in *Self-Portrait* don't attempt to resemble music by taking the false lead of "verbal music" and onomatopoeia in the manner of, say, Poe, or Edith Sitwell. Instead, they find a poetic equivalent of music—a kind of abstraction of argument and theme in which the reader follows a constantly evolving progression of mood, imagery, and tone, with sudden shifts and modulations, and a whole rainbow of emotive and conceptual sonorities; none of this logical or foreseeable and yet, at its best, embodying, in its engagement with chaos, an elusive, convincing necessity.

Strangely enough, but rightly, the poems make their music mainly out of visual materials: they are crowded with images, colors, silhouettes. Ashbery has the intense gaze of the child, the divine, or simply the poet, whose vision so absorbs him that the line between the visible world and the self begins to dematerialize, subject to fuse with object.

> The shadow of the Venetian blind on the painted wall,
> Shadows of the snake-plant and cacti, the plaster animals,
> Focus the tragic melancholy of the bright stare
> Into nowhere, a hole like the black holes in space.
>
> ["Forties Flick"]

None of this is to say that Ashbery's poems lack conceptual themes altogether. Argument, though not presented directly or logically, fuels and supervises the poetic proceedings, especially in the title poem. Because of the great ambiguity (surely more than seven kinds come into play) an Ashbery poem is likely to become a sort of *auberge espagnole,* to be furnished out in different schemes by every reader who stops with it; but that's usual even with less ambiguous poetry. Also, it's probably better to talk about the general *area* of meaning being explored, rather than about hard and fast aphoristic conclusions.

The phrase "tragic melancholy" from the above lines sums up for me the prevailing tone of the book. The tragedy arises from dilemmas of epistemology and solipsism; and Ashbery's characteristic response to those dilemmas is neither rage nor despair but melancholy—a melancholy well acquainted with terrible necessity but one whose most frequent gesture is a cosmic, valedictory shrug; things are like that, we have to move on. In good Pierrot fashion, Ashbery often transmutes melancholy into laughter; *Self-Portrait* is grandly comic. Anyone who has seen one of the old cartoons in which cat, coyote, or *luftmensch* walks over the edge of a cliff and navigates successfully until he perceives it was by blind faith alone knows that laughter may be metaphysical—and this scenario is one that occurs, varied and abstracted, in many of Ashbery's poems. Humor in *Self-Portrait,* if often crackerbarrel or camp, is also cosmic. To describe it, one wants to adapt Rilke's definition of beauty and say that, for Ashbery, laughter is the beginning of terror we're still just able to bear.

Three Poems made a kind of secular religion out of necessity: random and hopeless as our experience is, this book says, we are nonetheless "saved," and, in some sense, whatever is is OK. In *Self-Portrait* this benign vision has mostly been abandoned or temporarily supplanted by an agonized awareness of solipsism and radical uncertainty: Who or what is "I"? How is it that experience is nothing but ourselves and still, supremely, *not* ourselves? How can "I" be known to anyone else when "I" is already a conundrum to itself? To answer these questions is an unrealizable and therefore noble project. In a number of poems Ashbery performs the poetic equivalent of dead reckoning, whereby the subject moves from steppingstone to unsteady steppingstone, from bright, fading image to disembodied idea, from recollection to speculation, as if it all might lead to a conclusion, and not simply an ending. So much inconclusive striving, such a strenuous inertia, is very painful—all the more because the poems present the narrator as a kind of Tantalus who both believes and disbelieves in some final release, a privileged moment just about to occur in which all opposites will be united:

The pageant, growing ever more curious, reaches
An ultimate turning point. Now everything is going to be
Not dark, but on the contrary, charged with so much light
It looks dark, because things are now packed so closely together.
We see it with our teeth. And once this

Distant corner is rounded, everything
Is not to be made new again. We shall be inhabited
In the old way, as ideal things came to us,
Yet in the having we shall be growing, rising above it
Into an admixture of deep blue enameled sky and bristly gold
    stars.

["Voyage in the Blue"]

Privileged moments such as this one are presented as eva-
nescent; they solve nothing permanently and function largely
to make us realize the abjection of ordinary consciousness.

When we come to the end of one of these poems we would
feel dissatisfied at not having been provided with some kind
of resolution or wisdom if it weren't for the poems themselves, which are, at their best, enough. Two endings:

The night sheen takes over. A moon of cistercian pallor
Has climbed to the center of heaven, installed,
Finally involved with the business of darkness.
And a sigh heaves from all the small things on earth,
The books, the papers, the old garters and union-suit buttons
Kept in a white cardboard box somewhere, and all the lower
Versions of cities flattened under the equalizing night.
The summer demands and takes away too much,
But night, the reserved, the reticent, gives more than it takes.
                    ["As One Put Drunk into the Packet Boat"]

Yet we are alone too and that's sad isn't it
Yet you are meant to be alone at least part of the time
You must be in order to work and yet it always seems so
    unnatural
As though seeing people were intrinsic to life which it just might
    be
And then somehow the loneliness is more real and more human
You know not just the scarecrow but the whole landscape
And the crows peacefully pecking where the harrow has passed
                        ["Lithuanian Dance Band"]

So far I've avoided quoting from the title poem (which I
take to be the best in the volume). Extraordinary achievement is likely to be greeted with silence—you simply want to
point. Still, a few things can be said by way of guidelines for
the reader. "Self-Portrait in a Convex Mirror" is an extended
poem (reminding one again that in recent years, for whatever
reason, the best poems written in America are long poems),

and takes its title and subject from an early work of the Mannerist Francesco Parmigianino. The self-portrait is an "anamorphic" painting, that is, one that distorts normal perspective rendering by reproducing either a slant view of the subject or mediating it through non-plane reflecting surfaces such as cylindrical, conic, or convex mirrors. Examples of "slant" rendering (imagine looking at a movie screen from the first row) are found in the notebooks of Leonardo, and they almost always come into play in the trompe l'oeil effects in late-Renaissance and baroque ceiling frescoes. Jan van Eyck's *Arnolfini Marriage Group* (1434) and other Renaissance paintings include a convex mirror as a detail in a larger decor, but Parmigianino's self-portrait is the first—so far as I know, the only—portrait in a convex mirror.

Why did he paint himself this way? Why has Ashbery chosen this painting as a subject for poetic meditation? Call it happy accident, and then simply applaud the results—a painting of extraordinary psychological richness and a poem with passages like the following:

> But there is in that gaze a combination
> Of tenderness, amusement and regret, so powerful
> In its restraint that one cannot look for long.
> The secret is too plain. The pity of it smarts,
> Makes hot tears spurt; that the soul is not a soul,
> Has no secret, is small, and it fits
> Its hollow perfectly; its room, our moment of attention.

When I read this poem I'm reminded of a slide projector with a button-operated focus. A picture appears, sharp in outline; then another replaces it, out of focus—the vague forms, as they ooze toward clarity, suggest numerous possibilities, but, no, the picture is something different from anything we'd imagined, though the final image now seems inevitable. The next picture is blurred, too, and so engaging in its abstract form, we're tempted to leave it; but, reluctantly, we bring it into focus. When the show is over we realize that all the pictures shared something—they recorded a summer in Italy, or a trip to the National Gallery, or the building of a bridge.

I don't understand every line in "Self-Portrait," nor do I mind much; the coming and going of understanding as managed here is an interesting, involving experience. In any case, the freehand development of this poem's principal theme— that art is like a distorting mirror wherein we discover a more engaging, mysterious, and enduring image of ourselves than unmediated experience affords—is carried out with great assurance and variety; gradually, as one reads, the poem attains a supernatural, slow-motion grandeur seldom encountered in poetry or in any other medium:

> . . . A peculiar slant
> Of memory that intrudes on the dreaming model
> In the silence of the studio as he considers
> Lifting the pencil to the self-portrait.
> How many people came and stayed a certain time,
> Uttered light or dark speech that became part of you
> Like light behind windblown fog and sand,
> Filtered and influenced by it, until no part
> Remains that is surely you. Those voices in the dusk
> Have told you all and still the tale goes on
> In the form of memories deposited in irregular
> Clumps of crystals. Whose curved hand controls,
> Francesco, the turning seasons, and the thoughts
> That peel off and fly away at breathless speeds
> Like the last stubborn leaves ripped
> From wet branches? I see in this only the chaos
> Of your round mirror which organizes everything
> Around the polestar of your eyes which are empty,
> Know nothing, dream but reveal nothing.

Or, finally:

> . . . Is there anything
> To be serious about beyond this otherness

That gets included in the most ordinary
Forms of daily activity, changing everything
Slightly and profoundly, and tearing the matter
Of creation, any creation, not just artistic creation
Out of our hands, to install it on some monstrous, near
Peak, too close to ignore, too far
For one to intervene? This otherness, this
"Not-being-us" is all there is to look at
In the mirror, though no one can say
How it came to be this way. A ship
Flying unknown colors has entered the harbor.

3

World of the Interior: Boris Pasternak

Few critics consider Boris Pasternak the greatest twentieth-century poet writing in Russian; but readers who have never heard of any of the others know about him—that is, they know he was awarded the Nobel Prize in 1958 after the publication of *Doctor Zhivago*. It is his only novel. More powerful in its anti-Sovietism than anything by Nabokov (a better novelist but lesser poet), *Doctor Zhivago* was written not by an expatriate but by a member of the Union of Soviet Writers—which, however, promptly expelled him after the Nobel announcement.

Paradox often visited Pasternak's career, and not really as an uninvited guest. Like many artists of special intelligence he organizes his fictions according to it. "We depict people in order to cloak them with a climate—a climate, or, what is one and the same thing, with nature—with our passion. We drag the everyday into prose for the sake of the poetry of it. We draw prose into poetry for the sake of the music of it." The statement comes from *Safe Conduct,* his early auto-biographical memoir (1933), a brilliantly, perhaps too brilliantly written account of the genesis of a poet, something like Wordsworth's *The Prelude*. In his teens Pasternak first chose music as his vocation, largely because of the compelling example of Scriabin, who shone for him as a paragon of the artist and more particularly as a résumé of Russian culture. Then, doubts appeared. Though Scriabin praised his disciple's gifts, Pasternak gave up music because, he says, he lacked absolute pitch. It made no difference that Wagner, Tchaikovsky, and even Scriabin labored under the same disadvantage. He had made his decision, one presumably based on other factors for which lack of absolute pitch must have been only a synecdoche. Scriabin's last phase, incidentally, his efforts toward a synaesthetic fusion of all the arts, the staging of one huge performance called *Mysterium,* preferably in India, alienated Pasternak, and he described these late tendencies of Scriabin's as "ideas that reveal in a weary artist a previously concealed dilettante."

For a time, philosophy absorbed Pasternak's energies; he enrolled at the University of Marburg to study with the neo-Kantian Hermann Cohen and apparently distinguished himself. When the possibility of becoming a professor of philosophy loomed close, however, he rejected it. The decision coincided with the onrush of a first, unrequited love. He recounts how, after his courtship had been politely rebuffed, and his hopes dashed, the world of nature suddenly sprang into relief—nature understood not simply as pastoral, but the whole of physical, sensory reality, the earth, the sky, the city, in their varied colors, sounds, and smells, all of this felt as somehow consubstantial with the observer.

Pasternak returned to Russia by way of Italy, in particular, Venice. He seems by indirection to have found direction out. Italian Renaissance painting had a telling effect on Pasternak. His Italian journey was the concluding step that revealed to him his true vocation, as poet. For Pasternak, then, poetry may be seen as lying within the pentagram described by music, philosophy, love, physical nature, and Renaissance religious humanism in painting.

Pasternak's concern with musical analogies in verbal composition isn't unique to him, of course. In the twentieth century all the arts have aspired to the condition of music—with the frequent exception of music itself. The title poem of Pasternak's collection *Themes and Variations* (1923) goes farthest in the direction of musical form, still keeping, however, a modicum of paraphrasable content. Also, critics with an eye or an ear for it have described his collection of short stories as a classical four-movement symphony, the first story in sonata allegro form, the second a scherzo, and so forth.

Philosophy is present in Pasternak's writings—though Dr. Cohen would no doubt have considered Pasternak's statements as insufficiently clear or rigorous. Many of his formulations revolve around one central insight: when we perceive and feel the world intensely, we are the world, and we truly *exist,* in some sense eternally. This is a fertile point of departure for an artist, one found mainly among great poets and bad ones. In Pasternak, the theme finds beautiful, powerful expression. When, on the other hand, he ventures into historical or religious philosophy (mostly through the intermediary of characters in *Doctor Zhivago),* his footing is less sure; still, his statements are always interesting.

In Pasternak, the theme of love and verbal pictorialism intertwine precisely as the earlier quotation suggests. In love, we see truly, we receive a vision of the beloved in a "climate," a world; and this world proves to be interior, a heartland. As in Italian painting, the writer discovers poses and attitudes where the real and ideal coincide in one figure, a figure in an environment of radiant details.

Olga R. Hughes's *The Poetic World of Boris Pasternak,** is the best book in English about him. Clearly and concisely written, it would be valuable to both the expert and the layman. The book has generous excerpts from Pasternak's writings, the poetry given in both Russian and good English translation. Hughes argues that aesthetics is the most fruitful entry into Pasternak's writings, and her evidence is compelling. She points out that aesthetics in Pasternak shouldn't be distinguished from his principal themes—the two categories always overlap. The book, then, is organized as a kind of aesthetic and thematic index, singling out major phases of the poet's thought: the genesis and nature of poets and poetry, the relationship of art to reality, to time and "eternity," and,

*Princeton University Press, 1976.

finally, the poet's responsibility to society. In a rough way these topic headings, listed in order, trace the development of Pasternak's career and the shifts of emphasis during his creative lifetime.

The last phase begins with World War II, the period of Pasternak's most explicit concern with society and history. This period takes part of its character from Pasternak's repudiation of his earlier, elaborate style (described by Nina Berberova as "Soviet rococo"), in favor of plainer, more direct statement. He wrote *Doctor Zhivago* during this period and fewer poems; nevertheless, these are among his best, and especially the "poems of Yurii Zhivago," which conclude the novel. The novel itself, the work of one of the century's great modernists, paradoxically takes its place in the Russian tradition that moves from the nineteenth century and Tolstoy through Pasternak to the present and Solzhenitsyn. In this tradition, the Russian novelist is a kind of prophet, and his prophecies take the form of large historical frescoes that make palpable the dialectic of time and eternity. In *Doctor Zhivago,* a concrete referent for that dialectic is the counterpointed juxtaposition of prose and poetry in the novel's structure. Though the poems by placement have the last word, Pasternak shouldn't be viewed finally as either the Poet or the Prose Writer. He is, paradoxically, the relationship between the two.

4

Russian Encounters: Andrey Bely

A new Ice Age: so writers hailed the Soviet state as its power grew ever more centralized and its policies more rigid. Early Soviet programs included millions of political murders, these committed to accelerate an inevitable (so it was viewed) historical process that would usher in a state based on equity and freedom. No small number of those who fell victim to social progress were artists and writers. Some who could bear to abandon their country and language community fled to Germany, to France, to China, or to South America—a Russian diaspora that still continues. Of those who stayed behind, most gradually sank, or were pushed, into silence; only a few—Akhmatova, Ehrenburg, Pasternak—lived past middle age. The world community lost almost entirely what had emerged since the nineteenth century (along with the United States) as a supremely vital new tradition. Inspecting the roll of Russian artists active during the first two decades of the twentieth century (Chekhov, Malevich, Diaghilev, Blok, Mandelstam, Pasternak, Tsvetaeva, Meyerhold, Stravinsky, Bely, Kandinsky, Mayakovsky, dozens more), can we doubt that they would have dominated modern art and literature if their country had instituted a form of government allowing for free expression?

Andrey Bely's *The First Encounter** is one of the master-

---

*First published in 1921. Translated, with an introduction by Gerald Janaček, with notes and comments by Nina Berberova. Princeton University Press, 1979 (bilingual edition).

pieces of the early Soviet period; in fact, there is no long poem in Russian so great after this. Bely (Boris Nikolaevich Bugaev, 1880–1934) belongs, of course, to the Symbolist movement that first emerged in Russia during the 1890s. And, if his poems and novels continued to be printed in the U.S.S.R. until the mid-1930s, it was more a bureaucratic oversight than any real dovetailing of his concerns with those of the new regime.

The First Encounter, a record of his twentieth year (the year 1900) and the forces that shaped his aspirations as a writer, may be considered as Bely's *The Prelude.* The comparison gains force if the poem is taken in tandem with Bely's novel *Kotik Letaev* (completed in 1916, but not published as a book until 1922). This poem and novel belong to the "Moscow" cycle of his work, *Petersburg* (a novel) being the great example among his works concerned with the other chief Russian city. *Kotik Letaev,* like *The First Encounter,* is a study of the making of a poet; but it is prose fiction, and the autobiographical period covered, early childhood.

The volume includes a preface by Mr. Janaček and by Nina Berberova, the poet, slavicist, and author of an autobiographical memoir, *The Italics Are Mine.* Her preface discusses the use of iambic tetrameter in Russian poetry—it is the meter of *The First Encounter* and, in fact, of most of the great Russian poems since Pushkin. The nature and effect of metric variation within this frame are treated clearly and concisely; and Miss Berberova adds to this an instructive survey of the several modes of recitation practiced by Russian poets and actors since the nineteenth century. She has also provided exhaustive line notes for the poem.

The translation itself keeps close to the original iambic tetrameter, but dispenses almost entirely with rhyme. Bely's rhyme scheme for most of the poem was *abab,* with the customary alternating masculine and feminine rhymes, and no set strophic divisions. The translation reads smoothly and clearly, and there is every chance that it is literally accurate—the editors' acknowledgments mention that their version was checked by professors Simon Karlinsky and Robert Hughes, both excellent and scrupulous scholars.

The line notes make one constantly aware of how much verbal invention here belongs specifically to the Russian text of the poem; Bely's Symbolist aesthetic kept him close to the acoustics and grammar of his own tongue, and the effort to find analogues in other languages can never be entirely successful. Still, with a literally accurate translation and the notes, one can glimpse, as through a frosted pane, the marvel that the original poem must be. Divided into four parts, and with a prologue and epilogue, the poem is a synchronic reverie, playing freely among memories, speculations, and longings. Its nonnarrative organization resembles music, with verbal and thematic motifs standing as analogues to musical themes and harmonies.* The prologue is an invocation of the poetic afflatus, assimilated here to the Pentecostal descent of the Holy Spirit and the fiery gift of tongues. Part one recaptures Bely's sense of himself at age twenty, divided between scientific and mystical studies. The narrator's father is called "Dean Letaev," an indication of this poem's close relationship to the novel Kotik Letaev. The second section introduces a nonfictional personage, Mikhail Sergeevich Solovyov, and, more hazily, the latter's older brother, Vladimir. This Solovyov is the famous philosopher and poet, one of the principal influences on the Russian Symbolists Balmont, Bryusov, and of course Bely—though Solovyov himself disdained the movement. More urgent to him was the forging of his own syncretist religion, with elements borrowed from Eastern mysticism as well as Christianity. Vladimir Solovyov found a ready (if unsolicited) disciple in Bely, who was himself caught up in the project of uniting art, science, language mysticism, and syncretic religion in a new synthesis meant to dawn with the new century.

*On this aspect of the poem, see Simon Karlinsky's "Symphonic Structures in Andrej Belyj's 'Pervoe svidanie,'" California Slavic Studies, 6 (1971), p. 70.

The "encounter" referred to in the poem's title, then, is a first exposure to a man and a philosophical spirit. But it is also a romantic encounter with a woman and a physical entity. That woman is given the fictional name "Nadezhda Lvovna Zarina," but is based on an actual person, Margarita Morozova. (Her husband was the well-known Moscow businessman and patron of the arts, one of the earliest collectors in Russia of Bonnard and Matisse.) The romantic encounter between Bely and this representative of the Eternal Feminine—for so she is allegorized—is the subject of the poem's third section, perhaps the most brilliant verses Bely ever wrote. The setting is the Nobleman's Assembly Hall in Moscow, the occasion, a concert of one of the Beethoven symphonies. Bely deftly captures the heated atmosphere, the throngs crowding into the hall, the chatter, the costumes, the noise of the musicians' warm-up. From a distance he sees the beautiful Nadezhda, luminous and somehow at a spiritual remove from the hurly-burly around her. She becomes for Bely an avatar of Sophia, Heavenly Wisdom incarnate. Indeed it is her *fleshly,* material reality that the poem dwells on at length. By contrast Vladimir Solovyov's characterization is largely immaterial; he exists in the poem mostly as a phantom, a spirit. This antinomy is at the heart of Bely's thought: the spirit of order on the one hand, incarnate wisdom on the other. *(Incarnate* wisdom need not be a difficult notion—consider the very apt Shakespearean "ripeness," a metonymy based on fruition.)

In Bely's (and Solovyov's) syncretism, Christ is the Logos, and Nature (the Cosmos) is materialized wisdom. In her notes, Nina Berberova cites these comments from Bely's memoirs: "Transmuting logic into Christology and transmuting nature into Cosmos-Sofia, Solovyov unconsciously posited a purely anthroposophic theme, because the meeting of Cosmos-Sofia and Logos-Christ is a confrontation between the emotional and spiritual bases of human consciousness." Emotion and the senses belong to Cosmos-Sofia, and so the third section of the poem fills out Bely's notion of the Eternal Feminine by presenting her at a concert of *music,* the art of sound and feeling. (The realm of the Logos is of course language, philosophy, and poetry.) The description of the concert is a long tour de force, an effort to render, in words, musical impressions. By all accounts, Bely is more successful than any other Russian poet in this endeavor.

Part four follows the narrator out of the concert hall and into the streets and lanes of the winter city. There is a fleeting vision of the ghost of Vladimir Solovyov (who died in 1900); a visit to the chapel of the Blessed Virgin; and then the poem ends, concluding with a brief epilogue, dated "Pentecost and Whitmonday, 1921." The "encounters" have taken place, and Bely's *Prelude* has been accomplished.

I suggested earlier that *The First Encounter* should be read in tandem with *Kotik Letaev,* Bely's earlier spiritual autobiography. Among the features shared by the two works—a Moscow setting, the fictionalized "Dean Letaev," a cameo appearance of V. Solovyov—is the dualistic cosmology (used as an organizational principle) I have outlined. The sensibility of the novel's narrator is divided into "masculine" and "feminine" traits, these roughly grouped under the rubrics of "logical order" and "chaos." Gerald Janaček, in his introduction to the English translation of the novel, states that these attributes are symbolized acoustically by a thoroughly worked-out distribution of the phonemes k and l. One glance at the novel's title lends support to the proposition, since "Kotik" is the pet name bestowed by his mother on the first-person narrator of the poem, and "Letaev" is his surname (i.e., his father's name). Why these two phonemes? Because they correspond to Cosmos and Logos. "Kotik" means, by the way, "little cat," and emphasizes earthly, fleshly existence. "Letaev" contains the root *let,* which denotes "flight," a word associated with spiritual ascent throughout Bely's writings.

Another theme I wish to mention here and particularize is the very Belian preoccupation with "sparkles" or "a spark."

(The Russian word is *blesk.*) Among Bely's most characteristic effects are the shimmerings, glitterings, and coruscations of light. Lit-up crystal, snow, jewelry, crackling fires, all of these are common instances, but why should V. Solovyov be introduced in *Kotik Letaev* as "a sparkling but dangerous person"? And why does *The First Encounter* mention several times the play of sparkles in the lens of Mikhail Solovyov's eyeglasses? Apparently Bely associates sparkles with the "masculine" principle of spirit and thought—and of artistic inspiration as well. The last sentence of *Kotik Letaev* is, "My burnt-out torments are—this sparkle." The source of this image and theme is probably the writings of the Gnostics, whom Bely assuredly read, along with the theosophists, anthroposophists, and modern syncretists such as Solovyov. At least one direct allusion is made to Gnosticism in *The First Encounter,* and the last chapter of *Kotik Letaev* is titled, "A Gnostic." With this in mind, one does not hesitate to identify Bely's *blesk* as the Gnostic *pneuma* or spark of divine knowledge buried in all men and women imprisoned in the fallen material realm. Bely's version differs from orthodox Gnosticism in that he does not altogether repudiate the material cosmos; rather, he mythologizes it as a Mother, Sophia, Holy Wisdom incarnate, and seems content to live at a dualistic crossroads. That he manages to do so with high good humor is one of the odd features of this poet: he carries with him always an anarchic playfulness and drollery, even to the pinnacles of vision and ecstasy. We might tend to view this as a peculiarly Russian trait (and it is), but, if we reflect on other poets whose work bears the mark of Gnostic insights, we will conclude that it is not limited to one tradition. Much of Yeats's poetry keeps up an amused, Celtic good humor, even when deeply serious matters are being treated. The élan and sprightliness of Hart Crane's "For the Marriage of Faustus and Helen" might be another example. And if we consider the recent poetry of James Merrill, whose cosmology has an almost point-for-point resemblance to Bely's, it is apparent that the freewheeling Gnostic spirit is very much alive. This cannot really be surprising, given that the unstable set of transactions between matter and spirit stands among the central concerns of philosophy and art.

Given Bely's deep-grained dualism, it has to be expected that he, like Pasternak, would want to write prose as well as poetry. If, in poetry, emphasis must lie with the Logos, then prose is largely the realm of the Cosmos. What's more, the dialectic can be given a geographic dimension, in which the East is associated with spirit, and the West with matter. In *Petersburg,* Bely's greatest novel, * we can see many of his persistent concerns work themselves out under the auspices of a city understood as representing philosophical or spiritual categories that might not be grasped at first, even though a number of precedents can be named.

Actually, in those prime novels of city life—Balzac's Paris novels, *Bleak House, Ulysses, Mrs. Dalloway,* or *Manhattan Transfer*—the city becomes either a concrete embodiment of fate or a configuration of psyche, sometimes both. In Balzac the Faubourg Saint Honoré may represent the greed and vanity of his characters or, simply, capitalism. Nabokov singled out four great twentieth-century works of fiction—one for each of his languages—in these words: "My greatest masterpieces . . . are, in this order: Joyce's *Ulysses;* Kafka's *Transformation;* Bely's *Petersburg;* and the first half of Proust's fairy tale *In Search of Lost Time.*" All of these novels have urban settings, something that reflects the increasing urbanization of the earth and human consciousness and perhaps Nabokov's civilized perspective as well. But, of the four, only one takes the city name as its title; *Petersburg* is an eponymous novel. A city is its subject rather than any of its characters, who are present as constituents of a more important whole.

Petersburg appeared in three different versions (in 1916, 1922, and 1928) during Bely's lifetime, thereby bridging at

*Translated by Robert A. Maguire and John E. Malmstad. Indiana University Press, 1978.

least chronologically late Symbolism and the first Soviet phase of Russian literature. Aspects in it that might be interpreted as socialist-revolutionary made it eligible for reprinting as late as 1935; but its Symbolist aesthetic was judged less and less appropriate as Stalinism crystallized, censorship became more exacting, and the separation of aesthetics and the state a heresy, indeed, a crime. The name Petersburg itself was revised in 1924 to Leningrad, but no conceivable revision of Bely's novel could have transformed it into a work of socialist realism.

Petersburg is the culmination and the best example of the Russian Symbolist effort to accommodate itself to the novel. Clearly Symbolism and *poetry* are a better tandem, given Symbolism's strong anti-mimetic base. The novel, perhaps after cinema, has developed as the most thoroughgoing mimetic genre in Western culture. The peculiar success of *Petersburg* comes from its use of the tension between "realistic" and expressionistic modes of narrative. This is one in a series of polarizations that structure Bely's novel, polarizations he saw between the Western and Eastern elements in modern Russian culture. Petersburg was founded by Peter the Great in 1703 and given a Russian form of the Dutch for "Saint Peter's City." It has frequently been understood, then, as epitomizing the artificial grafting of Western European culture onto the native Eastern (even Mongol) stock. In Bely's novel, this city is associated in turn with a number of specifically Western evils—science and mathematics, urban dehumanization, bureaucracy and totalitarianism, cerebrality and repression of the body; and, on the aesthetic plane, naturalism. Against these the native virtues—physical vivacity, irrationality, religious consciousness, and an aesthetic of expressiveness, Symbolist or antinaturalist—stand in conflict.

According to this schema, Moscow is a synecdoche for things natively Russian—and Bely was a Muscovite. When he first began writing novels, he planned a trilogy, to be called *East or West,* in which the Petersburg-Moscow contrast would be central. In fact, the vestiges of his intentions were parceled out among separate novels, beginning with *The Silver Dove* and *Kotik Letaev,* and then *Petersburg* and a series of short pieces with Moscow settings. Bely saw that it was possible to treat the conflict within the confines of one of the two symbolic cities; perhaps he realized that the conflict was built into the structure of his own psyche—no purely "Eastern" artist could have assembled this almost mathematically structured work, notable for its naturalistic accuracy as much as for its phantasmagorical expressiveness. Whether the East-West schema will bear historical scrutiny is beside the point. Bely believed in his schema; at least, he used it as a structural principle in his work.

The character Apollon Apollonovich Ableukhov is the novel's triple-A Westernized Russian. His psychologically oppressed son Nikolai exhibits some of the opposing Eastern tendencies; others are distributed among Nikolai's revolutionary-terrorist-mystical associates who have decided, arbitrarily, that he must kill his father (by means of a little bomb concealed in a sardine tin). The action hovers around this simple plot line, with one secondary narrative, the farcical account of troubles in the marriage of Sofia Petrovna and her husband Likhutin. An unpromising framework, but Bely weaves on it a tapestry of great power, strangeness, and beauty.

Among the novel's symbolic emblems are the bronze equestrian statue of Peter the Great, familiar to readers of Pushkin; the various sectors of the city, with their political or literary associations; and the geometry of the city plan at large. The polarizations outlined earlier find a counterpart in the novel's dominant color scheme: the shimmering pearl-gray tonality of Pushkin's Petersburg Bely reduces to a flat grayness, with black accents, standing for all that is Western. Eastern energies are emblematized as red—in fact, Nikolai Apollonovich appears from time to time throughout the novel clad in a red domino that conceals his face and allows him to wander through the city as a sort of Lord of Misrule bent on disruption and shocking the bourgeoisie.

Other emblematic oppositions include those between plane geometry (or straight-line geometrical figures) and solid or curved-line figures—the square as opposed to the sphere, say, or more accurately, the *expanding* sphere. This recurs often in the novel and is sometimes assimilated to the human heart. Bely seems, not unnaturally, to link expansion to inspiration and freedom. (This same notion had been used in the opening section of *The First Encounter*, which depicts a series of expansions powered by the heat and fire of poetic emotions.) If Bely's allegory is to be worked out resolutely, we have to see the little terrorist sardine tin to stand as much for the liberating spirit of poetry and the Logos as for the instrument of revolutionary change. Bely's Soviet censors obviously lacked allegorical skills, a blind spot that has continued to allow for extra meanings in Soviet literature written since the Stalinist period.

I don't pretend, myself, to have understood all that can be found in *Petersburg*. Because of Bely's practice of attributing conceptual or emotional meaning to phonemes, not all of his intentions are available to those who must read the novel in translation. And he uses literary allusion as part of his dramatic and philosophical structure. To have caught echoes of Pushkin's *The Bronze Horseman* and *The Stone Guest* or Gogol's *The Overcoat,* or some of Dostoevsky's or Tolstoy's novels, doesn't guarantee having caught *all* the allusions to fiction and poetry Bely has made, or being certain how he means them to be interpreted in context. But Bely's overall aim seems clear, and he offers many incidental pleasures along the way toward building his spiritual edifice. *Petersburg,* along with Bely's Moscow writings, is an important literary milestone in that persistent theme of Russian culture, the search for a national identity.

5

The Anglo–Italian Relationship: Eugenio Montale

They read Faulkner in Prague; Kafka in Paris; Colette in Missouri. Scholars of twentieth-century literature must be prepared to compare; and it's something more than frivolous to play the "naturalization" game—Pound is our best Italian, Stevens our best French poet, and so on. In Italy the characteristic twentieth-century French poet would no doubt be Ungaretti; and the characteristic English poet is Montale. One can begin by observing the heavy sprinkling of English words, phrases, and place names in his poetry and then go on to more central facts such as Montale's having traveled often in England; his translating Shakespeare, Marlowe, Keats, Melville, Hawthorne, Dickinson, Hardy, and T. S. Eliot; or his critical writings on Pound, Joyce, Hopkins, and Hemingway. Of course, an Italian-English affinity, centering mostly around readings of Dante, has functioned in the opposite direction since the Victorians and contributed to the formation of many of those writers in English that attracted Montale.

Rather than trying to find a way through the labyrinth of reciprocity, I want to isolate some of the shared features in this Anglo-Italian tradition. They include a high seriousness of purpose and tone; a belief in the centrality of love, human or divine, to experience and to the artistic experience; an interest in the "everydayness" of life, mundane reality transformed by imaginative contexts into something radiant and resonant; and a sense of poetry as speech and voice, not merely writing. Along with these predilections go a few negatives—dislike of "art for art's sake," grandiloquence, cynicism, or the grotesque.

These points of contact partly account for Montale's having become the best-known modern Italian poet in the English-speaking world. He was that even before his Nobel Prize award in 1975. As early as 1928 he published a poem ("Arsenio," translated by Mario Praz) in *Criterion,* then still under Eliot's editorship. Translations of selected poems began appearing in England in the fifties. If Robert Lowell serves as an index of our interests, the fact that ten of his fourteen Italian translations are based on Montale poems is telling. Also, Montale attracted the attention of F. R. Leavis, a critic who was seldom moved to praise contemporary or foreign writers; and, in the U.S., a half-dozen volumes of translations are in print, which is the case for no other modern Italian poet.

From the evidence, there are ears among us to hear Montale; but we apparently lack tongues to explain him. I know of only one book on Montale in English, a fairly useful study by G. Singh. Apart from Leavis's, the articles that have appeared are brief, specialized, and not very substantial. Why this critical neglect? Is it because Montale has seldom been translated well? That may be part of the answer, but there must be other reasons.

Despite the affinity outlined above, Montale still belongs to the continental European tradition. Since the nineteenth century, French, Italian, German, and Spanish poetry has tolerated a much higher degree of difficulty, of "hermeticism," than has English or American poetry. To the extent that Eliot was influenced by the French Symbolists he was labeled "obscure"; and no doubt the same holds for Stevens and Crane. Also, continental philosophy, very much at odds with the English empirical tradition, has had a continuous influence on the poetry written in those countries—and the influence is often reciprocal (Goethe and Nietzsche, for example, or Hölderlin and Heidegger). The result is that the metaphysical or dialectical concerns of a good deal of continental poetry, including Montale's, are apt to strike English readers as misplaced, forced, even unreal.

Montale was never altogether a "hermetic" poet, certainly not in his first book. The poems in *Ossi di seppia* (*Cuttlefish Bones*), published in 1925, decipher fairly easily. Many of the poems are taken up with description, sometimes of interiors but more often of landscapes or seascapes. Montale develops the relationship between narrator and environment in a peculiar way: the two exist in reciprocity, a kind of spiritual symbiosis that Ruskin would have put under his rubric of the "pathetic fallacy." We no longer find this approach scandalous; in any case, Montale's landscapes are notable for their concretion, their vivid particulars. The poems in the sequence "Mediterraneo" form a series of meditations on the sea at the shores of the Cinque Terre, in the Liguria where Montale spent his childhood summers. *Mare,* the sea, has masculine gender in Italian. Montale addresses it as "Father," "Antico," a titanic force indifferent to men but nonetheless the ultimate source of life and life rhythms, and therefore of poetry too. A second natural phenomenon that preoccupies the poet is sunlight, the noonday meridional glare, which annihilates everything except "una certezza: la luce" ("one certainty: light"). He invokes the sunflower as his nearest emblem because it is "maddened with light." Under the relentless noonday sun the poet says,

> Bene lo so; bruciare,
> questo, non altro, è il mio significato.

> Well I know: to burn,
> this, and nothing else, is my significance.

Apart from Camus's *L'Envers et l'endroit,* a collection of poetic essays on the Mediterranean under the North African sun, or perhaps also Valéry's "Cimetière marin," I know of no comparable treatment of this subject matter.

Throughout the Mediterranean sequence and indeed through many of the other poems as well runs the theme of desire for "un evento impossibile," a moment of transcendence or escape from fatality, limitation, the bondage of mortality. The poet tries to imagine some "loophole" in nature,

> il punto morto del mondo, l'anello che non tiene,
> il filo da disbrogliare che finalmente ci metta
> nel mezzo di una verità.

> the dead point of the world, the link that doesn't hold,
> the thread to disentangle which might set us at last
> in the middle of a truth.

Moments of escape or transcendence are presented here and in such poems as "Quasi una fantasia" as hypothetical, mere supposition, always in the future. They are never to be realized; or perhaps the poet knows that their sole chance for realization lies in poetry, as hypothetical, imagined experience.

On the other hand, Montale presents as actual and palpable "il male di vivere," ("the evil of living"), "questa tortura senza nome," ("this nameless torment"), the "fissità gelida" ("frozen fixity") of human suffering. The Ligurian landscape, sun-beaten, rocky, desiccated, with theatrical vistas of the sea and precipitous cliffs, seems to echo sympathetically the theme of spiritual torment. (Montale finds a verbal equivalent for that landscape, a gravelly, heavily consonanted speech, as in these phrases from "Meriggiare pallido e assorto,": "schiocchi di merli, frusci di serpi . . . tremuli scricchi di cicale dai calvi picchi.") Human love would seem to be for Montale the best response to the "male di vivere." But it is seldom presented in its happiest aspect. Instead, almost all of his poems on love deal with estrangement, the sense of betrayal and loss. So true is it that the majority of Montale's poems are built around the theme of love that he could be reproached for repetitiveness; however, this is the one form of repetitiveness that most readers are readily disposed to forgive.

A good part of genius lies in the careful working out of detail. *Ossi di seppia* makes the impression it does not only because of its serious thematic concerns but also because of Montale's careful craftsmanship. I offer seven lines from "Caffè a Rapallo," remarkable for their sound, imagery, and economical scene-setting:

> Natale nel tepidario
> lustrante, truccato dai fumi
> che svolgono tazze, velato
> tremore di lumi oltre i chiusi
> cristalli, profili di femmine
> nel grigio, tra lampi di gemme
> e screzi di sete. . . .

> Christmas in the tepidarium,
> gleaming, masked by fumes
> rising from cups, veiled trembling
> of lights beyond the closed
> panes, profiles of women
> in the dusk rayed through by gems
> and whispering silks. . . .

[translated by Irma Brandeis and James Merrill in *Selected Poems*, New Directions, 1965]

The steamy atmosphere of the café in wintertime, the drop-streaked panes, profiles, and silks are beautifully captured here; and one feels that the play of sibilant and fricative consonants as well as the repeated vowel *i* somehow adds to the total impression.

Consider also the following two lines from "Cigola la carrucola" ("The Pulley Creaks"), or rather consider what happens *between* the two lines. The narrator has drawn a pail of water from a well and thinks he sees something in it:

> Trema un ricordo nel ricolmo secchio,
> nel puro cerchio un'immagine ride.

> A memory trembles in the brimming pail,
> in that pure circle an image smiles.

I hope my translation captures the process of abstraction at work here—a sort of "Platonization" that occurs between the two lines, thrown into relief by the chiasmus or transposition of the two objects of attention. Phenomenon is simplified into idea, a procedure similar to certain sculpture series by Matisse and Brancusi, which begin with naturalistic forms and purify these step by step into geometric reductions.

To return to the issue of hermeticism: it's apparent from the phrases so far cited that Montale is very much a poet for the ear, probably even more so than for the eye. His first ambition was to perform in opera, and he studied voice seriously. Preparation for the role of Valentin in Gounod's *Faust* was nearly completed when his teacher died. Montale decided to pursue voice studies no further, and something more private than his teacher's death must have determined that decision. In any case, he was always interested in music; until his death he served as opera critic for *Corriere della sera*. Not surprisingly, his poems show a high degree of sonorous organization. I suspect that his concern for pure sound has sometimes worked against clear expression of content; but I also find that reading difficult passages aloud eases the uncomfortable feeling of not having understood. Nearly all of his poems contain passages virtuosic from the standpoint of sound alone. An example from an untranslated poem:

> Lunge risuona un grido: ecco precipita
> il tempo, spare con risucchi rapidi

> tra i sassi, ogni ricordo è spento; ed io
> dall'oscuro mio canto mi protendo
> a codesto solare avvenimento.
>
> ["Crisalide"]

After the resounding cry (with a play on *ecco,* which means "behold" but sounds like *eco* ["echo"]), the tempo is literally precipitate, the lines sharply and irregularly accented except for the perfect iambics of the penultimate line; and the whole passage plays pitch-and-toss with the consonants *s* and *r* and the vowels *a* and *o.* The influence of Dante on Montale as to tone and content has often been remarked; we might also discover an influence at the level of sonics, instancing lines such as Virgil's reproach to Charon in the third Canto of the *Inferno:* "'Caron, non ti crucciare: / vuolsi così colà dove si puote/ciò che si vuole, e più non dimandare.'"

Here is a second example, also not yet translated:

> La tua voce è quest'anima diffusa.
> Su fili, su ali, al vento, a caso, col
> favore della musa o d'un ordegno,
> ritorna lieta o triste. Parlo d'altro,
> ad altri che t'ignora e il suo disegno
> è là che insiste *do re la sol sol* . . .

This is the second of two stanzas in one of Montale's "Motets." The first, broader and more measured, might be compared to an operatic *cavatina.* The second picks up the tempo, especially at line two, a lightsome passage in three-quarter time much like the *cabaletta* that usually follows a *cavatina.* That the subject of the poem is the beloved's voice singing the little *solfège* at the end makes my characterization of the poem perhaps less arbitrary.

The "Motets" appear in Montale's second volume, *Le occasioni,* published in 1932. The tendency toward hermeticism is here at its strongest. Two factors contributed to this, one external, the other a personal, aesthetic *parti pris.* Montale was altogether out of sympathy with the Fascist régime. Although his poetry attempted to engage the sordid realities of the time, it could only voice an indirect protest. The danger of repression was real; for their polemical writings against Fascism Gobetti was murdered and Gramsci imprisoned. As it was, Montale was removed from his position at the Vieusseux Library in Florence for refusing to join the Fascist party. Montale's sympathies are clear enough in poems such as "A Liuba che parte" and "Dora Markus," both addressed to young Jewish women displaced by the gathering storm. His hatred for the stifling political atmosphere can be decoded in the symbol of the death's-head moth that makes an ominous visit to the family home in the poem "Vecchi versi." His sense of loss and confusion is apparent in the quasi-Petrarchan projection of the image of the beloved onto an immense fresco of domestic and international disruption, as in the difficult but powerful poem "Nuove stanze." Indeed, the overall tone of frustration and bitterness in Le *occasioni* may be understood as an emotional emblem for Montale's attitude toward the political and social conditions in Fascist Italy.

But Montale's hermeticism in these poems has a purely aesthetic aspect as well. He had become dissatisfied with the merely expository element in poetry—he wanted essence and not accident. "Occasions" are precisely what one seldom finds in Le *occasioni*. Instead Montale presents emotional significance and psychic texture as almost the whole of the poem—expression rather than representation, the lamp rather than the mirror. The method is at its purest and most successful in the "Motets," twenty brief lyrics centering again on the theme of estrangement from the beloved, a figure of both human and divine stature. This approach to poetic form allows for great condensation and therefore great power; but the poems are undeniably difficult. I quote the sixteenth of the "Motets" in full, translated by Irma Brandeis in *Selected Poems:*

(Il fiore che ripete
dall'orlo del burrato
non scordati di me,
non ha tinte più liete né più chiare
dello spazio gettato tra me e te.

Un cigolio si sferra, ci discosta,
l'azzurro pervicace non ricompare.
Nell'afa quasi visible mi riporta all'opposta
tappa, già buia, la funicolare.)

The flower that repeats
from the edge of the crevasse
forget me not,
has no tints fairer or more blithe
than the space tossed here between you and me.

A clank of metal gears puts us apart.
The stubborn azure fades. In a pall of air
grown almost visible, the funicular
carries me to the opposite stage. The
                              dark is there.

Sonority is the first casualty in translation, hence we lose here the lovely composition of vowel *e* assonances in the original's first stanza; but some of the rough metallic noise of the second has been brought over in the translation. The funicular may or may not have an actual referent; what's important is the condition of separation, emphasized by the stanzaic break. The relationship between the "you" and "me" of the poem is rendered by a flower with clear associations—the forget-me-not, named in the Italian only by its message. Its color becomes an emblem for the feelings between the couple, and this is likewise rendered as having a spatial dimension—a private emotional "space" reminiscent of Rilke's use of the word *Raum*. Physical separation threatens that space (the threat in retrospect is apparent—the flower grows on the

edge of a "crevasse," and the danger is underlined by an astute enjambment). Removed from the beloved, the poet feels
the color fade; air, that is, mere physical space, becomes "almost visible"; and darkness has risen.

This is perhaps a good point to take up Montale's special
use of the "you" (*tu* in all poems except "Tentava la vostra
mano" and "Crisalide," which use *voi;* he never uses the formal *lei.*) The "you" of the poems may be an actual woman,
or an actual woman apotheosized by "dolcestilnovism" in
the manner of Petrarch or Dante as a divine principle. Or, the
poet may also be addressing himself as "you," in one or more
aspects. Or a whole environment may be so addressed.
Sometimes more than one of these categories is intended
within a single poem, a procedure often leaving the reader in
confusion—and not unhappily; there is a rich sense of association and layered meaning, metamorphoses unfolding in a
house of mirrors. In a late poem called "Il tu" Montale has
accounted for this special usage by instancing the many selves
contained in one self, some of these understood, I think, as
inanimate—that is, until the poet breathes life and voice into
them. Apart from the usefulness of this technique in provid-
ing smooth though transitionless movement from impulse to
impulse within a poem, it also contributes to the personal
"speechly" quality of the poems, so that we get a conversation, not just a text. In opera there are few soliloquies—most
arias are addressed to other personages and so constitute part
of the drama.

The most impressive single example of Montale's use of
the *tu* comes in "La casa dei doganieri" ("The Shorewatchers'
House"). Again, it is a poem built around the theme of estrangement, and difficult to paraphrase. One of its main ger-
minative impulses is an interplay of analogical images
connected to the phenomenon of spinning objects or bobbins
that wind up a thread. (Had Montale been reading about
Yeats's gyres?) In an already dizzying welter of images—
storms, twirling weathervanes, bobbins—the *tu* appears and
seems alternately to refer to a "you" and the poet himself.

The inward spiraling of subjective imagination is countered with an occasional objective image, such as the striking presentation of the tanker out against the horizon, a tiny light under the nighttime storm. The diction and rhythms of the poem are rough, stormy, fortissimo passages of brass and percussion, with a final decrescendo for strings and woodwinds. The performance of a master. I have other favorites in *Le occasioni,* which I will simply mention rather than analyze: the "Carnevale di Gerti," remarkable for its inventiveness and kaleidoscopic play of imagery; "Nel parco di Caserta," mysterious and disquieting; and the lovely "Tempi di Bellosguardo," classically Tuscan in feeling and expression.

In 1943, doubting that it would pass censorship, Montale published in Switzerland a small group of poems called *Finisterre.* The opening poem, "La bufera" ("The Storm"), has as epigraph some verses of Agrippa d'Aubigné, reproaching the rulers for their indifference to their subjects, whom they persecuted rather than served. The "storm" in question is of course the disastrous war and condition of civil injustice in Italy. The poems finally appeared in Italy after peace was declared, first in a limited edition by themselves, and then as the first section of *La bufera e altro* (The Storm and Other Poems), published by Mondadori in 1956. Montale considered this volume his most solid collection. Not everyone agrees with that judgment, but there are poems in it quite unlike any that had gone before. The discourse, in general, is ampler, less distilled; a warm, humanistic glow, rather like the light in Rembrandt's late paintings, pervades poems such as "Voce giunta con le folaghe," a moving recreation of the poet's late father; or "Proda di Versilia," a backward glance at his childhood and the seacoast that fostered so many of his poems.

The fifth section of the book opens with "Iride," a poem addressed to a woman who is at once an actual person, a flower (perhaps also a butterfly), and a divine principle, the classical Iris, messenger of the gods and associated with the rainbow. For Montale she represents the eternal spirit of sacrifice, especially as exemplified in Christian doctrine. This figure is invoked across space and time; she has left Italy to serve as an emissary to colder climates in the North, thereby recapitulating the itinerary of early Christian missionaries. By contrast, the closing poem of this same section is "L'anguilla" ("The Eel"), a poem on a natural creature that makes the reverse pilgrimage, from the Baltic Sea to tiny ditches and creeks in Italy, its breeding grounds. I have never seen the two poems discussed in tandem, but Montale has obviously intended them to be juxtaposed, perhaps seeing the complementarities of north and south, human (or divine) and natural, spiritual and physical, as constituting some desirable whole. The final lines of "L'anguilla" are:

> l'iride breve, gemella
> di quella che incastonano i tuoi cigli
> e fai brillare intatta in mezzo ai figli
> dell'uomo, immersi nel tuo fango, puoi tu
> non crederla sorella?

> brief rainbow [iris], twin
> to that within your lashes' dazzle, that
> you keep alive, inviolate, among
> the sons of men, steeped in your mire—in this
> not recognize a sister?
> [translated by John Frederick Nims in *Selected Poems*]

And in the poem "Piccolo testamento" ("Little Testament"), Montale cites the iris as the only legacy he can leave behind of a "faith that was opposed, / a hope that burned slower / than a hardwood log on the hearth." The poem closes with some quiet affirmations, given characteristically as a series of negatives.

> Ognuno riconosce i suoi: l'orgoglio
> non era fuga, l'umiltà non era

vile, il tenue bagliore strofinato
laggiù non era quello di un fiammifero.

Everyone recognizes his own: that pride
was not evasion, that humility was not
base, that feeble light struck
down there was not the flame of a match.
[my translation]

Nel nostro tempo (In Our Time), a book of essays published in 1972, sums up Montale's views on recent social and literary developments at home and abroad. He says: "To participate in a collective cry, in a universal *no*, seems to be the sole ambition of the modern artist." Here for the first time Montale dissociated himself from modern art. If his own affirmations were guarded and won with difficulty, nonetheless he made them. Reading these prose pieces Montale wrote in the sixties and early seventies, one quickly understands that he was squarely opposed to several currents in recent history— mass and pop culture; the political developments in Italy; the aesthetics of shock and confrontation; and the new linguistic, structuralist criticism.

Not many of us would rush to disagree with him on these issues; but for the poetry the results of his disaffection with contemporary reality seem to have been bad, on the whole. In 1970 Montale published *Satura* (a Latin word suggesting the satiric treatment of a variety of topics). A large number of the poems are essayistic in impulse and ironic in tone. To read many of them at a sitting is fatiguing; except for the frequent display of wit and humanity, most of the poems seem un-Montalean. Fortunately none of these strictures applies to the splendid *Xenia*, which opens the book. In two parts, each with fourteen brief numbered sections, the sequence is a brilliant, cinematic evocation of Montale's late wife, nicknamed Mosca. The poet darts from scene to distinct scene, sketching in the features of an idiosyncratic character, all of this carried out with brevity, wit, and a sane tenderness. The poems peculiarly combine naturalistic detail, dialogue, reverie, comedy, bereavement, and a meditative frame of mind akin to prayer. It is this sequence that Leavis has written about, accurately comparing it to the collection of lyrics Hardy wrote in 1912 and 1913 after the death of his wife. Montale ends the poem by conflating the personal catastrophe with the flood that ravaged Florence in the mid-sixties. He mentions the loss of personal possessions and concludes:

> Anch'io sono incrostato fino al collo se il mio
> stato civile fu dubbio fin dall'inizio.
> Non torba m'ha assediato, ma gli eventi
> di una realtà incredibile e mai creduta.
> Di fronte ad essi il mio coraggio fu il primo
> dei tuoi prestiti e forse non l'hai saputo.

> I,
> too, am encrusted up to the neck
> since my civil status was doubtful from the outset.
> It isn't mud has besieged me, but the events
> of an incredible reality which was never believed.
> In the face of these my courage was the first
> of your gifts and perhaps you didn't know it.

> [translated by G. Singh in *New Poems,*
> New Directions, 1976]

Montale's fifth collection of poems, *Diario del '71 e del '72,* appeared in 1973. While the dates of composition as given in the table of contents make it clear that the book is not precisely a chronological poetic journal for the two years, even so it does give that impression when read in sequence. The poems are brief for the most part, as if casually jotted down in response to various kinds of stimuli. They resemble the previous collection in being more accessible than the earlier "hermetic" work, but the tone has softened slightly; there is less bitterness than in *Satura,* less irony.

Finally, in 1981, a last collection of Montale's poetry, *Altri versi e poesie disperse,* was published in Italy, appearing in America three years later as *Otherwise: Last and First Poems,* skillfully translated and edited by Jonathan Galassi. Some of Montale'e earlier power reappears in this collection, not only in the poems from the years 1918–28 never before collected, but also in the new poems. The sharpness and dismissiveness of the older Montale is present throughout; but many of the poems are based on anecdotal subjects, and it is Montale's mastery at weaving circumstance and comment together that makes the most striking impression here. "The truth" and Montale's impatience with it seem to have one substance: the poet's highest tribute to reality is to include his actual, low estimate of it—because such are the facts. An idealist is always forced into paradox, and Montale's paradoxes are among the most painful in poetry.

> Suppongo che a qualcuno, a qualcosa convenga
> l'attributo di essente. In quel giorno eri tu.
> Ma per quanto, ma come? Ed ecco che rispunta
> la nozione esecrabile del tempo.
>
> ["Quartetto"]

> I suppose, someone, something, deserves
> the epithet of being. On that day it was you.
> But for how long, but how? And here again
> the execrable idea of time resurfaces.
>
> ["Foursome"]

II

TWO NOVELISTS

6

Time to
Read Proust

Delayed for half a century, why shouldn't the Age of Proust begin now? Partly because this age has become so eclectic that no single author could lend it a name; and partly because Joyce still seems to hold, particularly for us Anglo-Saxons and Celts, some formal insights worth developing. *Finnegans Wake* of course bowed more than once in Proust's direction, not just by noting that "the prouts will invent a writing" and mentioning "swansway" but also by adapting Proust's clockwise-circular narrative form and extending the principle of involuntary recall to the entire history of our "collective unconscious." The United Nations inclusiveness of *Finnegans Wake* and its oneiric Esperanto incidentally guarantee it an audience among French linguistic-textual critics; but this privileged position it must share with *A la recherche du temps perdu,* if with no other twentieth-century novel.

The rapidest glance backward makes clear why the Proust era didn't begin in the 1920s for either French or English-language literature. The complete *Ulysses* appeared first—published in cosmopolitan Paris under the benevolent regard of an important group of cosmopolite writers. A French translation was undertaken immediately. Also, Joyce was still alive, still writing. Even when the *Recherche* appeared in 1927—posthumously—it seemed like the end, not the beginning, of something. The wind in French writing had shifted toward Breton's Surrealism, on one hand, and then

Nietzschean thought (atheist, Dionysian, agonized), developed in fiction by Gide, Céline, Malraux, Sartre, and Camus. Proust never lacked readers but still had no disciples among his younger contemporaries up to the apostolic succession. In England, the vogue for Proust had begun even before the twenties among writers who read French, but did not grow widespread until C. K. Scott Moncrieff's translation began appearing. Scott Moncrieff died in 1930 before taking up *Le Temps retrouvé*. This last volume was translated by "Stephen Hudson" (Sidney Schiff) in England and by Frederick A. Blossom in the United States, and then once more by Andreas Mayor. To what degree English writers like Forster, Woolf, Waugh, Bowen, Greene, and Green were influenced by Proust, scholars can debate; however small that influence, it has still weighed more heavily with the English than with the Americans or even the French.

It's not surprising that the English felt an affinity with the work of an admiring reader of Shelley, Ruskin, George Eliot, and Hardy; by the same argument, Americans could expect to feel strong sympathies with this French disciple of Emerson, once they paused to notice the overlap of Romantic philosophy and retrospective temperament in Proust. The length of the *Recherche* and its language may have been a barrier; but those who understand the importance of a great work will always answer its requirements; and those who cannot read French now have an adequate translation of the greatest novel written in the twentieth century so far.

To say "adequate" instead of "superb" needs justifying; but first I should retell the story of this translation. After Scott Moncrieff's version appeared (I use one name to designate the three hands that worked on that version because Schiff and Mayor tried to imitate Scott Moncrieff's style and texture in their renderings of the last volume), most readers praised its accuracy and its sensitive, idiomatic English. Yet others disliked the archaizing, "Edwardian" sound of Scott Moncrieff and pointed out inaccuracies, euphemisms, and bowdlerizations. Those objections, however, led to no attempts at retranslation. Meanwhile, a new French edition of the novel appeared in 1954, published by the Bibliothèque de la Pléiade. The Pléiade edition corrected textual errors, added valuable passages discovered by the editors in the jumble of Proust's manuscripts, supplied textual notes and variants, and included both a plot résumé with page references and a place and name index for the gigantic work. Now, more than twenty years later, we have an English version in conformity with the current French Proust. The new edition, prepared by Terence Kilmartin and published in three volumes, follows the Pléiade text, with the new interpolations tipped in unobtrusively and the same plot résumés added at the end of each volume, though without a place and name index. Some of the textual variants appear in an appendix; and the text notes, different from the Pléiade's, have been composed with English and American readers in mind.

As he explains in his prefatory note, Kilmartin has done not an entirely new translation but a *rifacimento* of Scott Moncrieff, with additions from the Pléiade newly translated. He hoped to satisfy both admirers and detractors of the earlier version, and I think at least the admirers of Scott Moncrieff will be satisfied; this new version hews closely to the earlier. But the detractors? Despite some updatings laid over the old text, the prose still sounds 1890s–ish. For a second translator to retain Scott Moncrieff's "the morrow" as a translation for "le lendemain," or "frightfully good" for "très bien" is not to measure up to the proclaimed intention of modernizing the text, and these tokens can stand for a problem apparent throughout Kilmartin's version. Proust doesn't sound moldy in French; why should he in English? Also, American readers must be prepared for English spellings—"programme," "connexion," "labour"—though I notice, too, a few American "judgments" and "acknowledgments" scattered inconsistently throughout. Tiny flaws, surely; they deserve mention only because the fanfare around this new edition, so handsomely bound and printed, so expensive, so heavy and unwieldy, led me to expect perfection.

Considering that fanfare and that expense, what accounts for the much more serious problem of persistent mistranslation? Kilmartin corrected some of Scott Moncrieff's errors—bravo. Without sorting out who first perpetrated the errors that remain, I would still say the new text should have none at all and am baffled that more checking wasn't done. Reading the first sentence, for example, I was disappointed to see that Scott Moncrieff's mistranslation had been let stand: "For a long time I used to go to bed early." Among several possibilities for translating the most famous decasyllabic sentence in French fiction, this is the least acceptable. "Longtemps, je me suis couché de bonne heure." Kilmartin has justified the retention as a way of making the verb tense—*passé composé*—blend with the overall imperfect tense of the opening paragraph. But Proust knew grammar and had an acute syntactic ear. The little jolt between the temporal suspension of the first sentence (comparable to verbs in the aorist aspect in Greek) and the flowing, imperfective aspect of the second is part of the intended effect and should be left. "For a long time now, I have gone to bed early," comes closer to the original. (Then the pluperfect tense Kilmartin imposes on the second sentence would have to go; but he could easily have fixed that.)

The grammar of this translation is sometimes substandard. "Cannot help but" is too careless a locution to use for so exact and formal a writer as Proust. I wonder if others object to this sentence: "And nothing reminds me so much of the monthly parts of *Notre Dame de Paris,* and of various books by Gérard de Nerval, that used to hang outside the grocer's door at Combray, than does, in its rectangular and flowery border, supported by recumbent river-gods, a 'personal share' in the Water Company." "So much" should be changed to "more strongly" or else "than" to "as"; Proust's sentence uses the right connectives, and the translator has only to follow them.

Among the dozens of wrong choices I noticed before hopes for a superb translation waned, I will mention one; and perhaps this anecdote will help explain it. On my first trip to France, the language program I had enrolled in billeted its students in French homes—room, board, and conversation. This was in Avignon, and my hosts lived three miles outside town. The locals called the house, with modest irony, "le château"—a solidly built pile about 150 years old, with a classic pediment over the front entrance (seldom used) and bean fields that came up to within a few paces of the back door. The ceilings were high, the furniture unremarkable. My first evening there I sat down to talk with my hosts over a thimbleful of homemade *pastis*. Twenty years old and still disoriented, I meant to learn to speak French. I turned to the smiling, florid gentleman (wearing a leather jacket but no tie) who gave me my drink, and asked him "what he did." "Ma foi, je suis paysan," he laughed. France is not nineteenth-century Rumania; it's thoughtless to translate *paysan* as "peasant." There are no peasants in France, no more than there are in England. If I had been Kilmartin, I would have ruled out the obvious and then chosen among "farmer," "yeoman," "bumpkin," or perhaps "farmhand," depending on context.

I have to object to another detail, not a translation but an addition: Scott Moncrieff's subtitle "Overture," for the first fifty pages of the novel, should not have been retained. Proust gave the section no title; and, while the translator's argument for doing so has merit, it covers only half the case. Stressing the musical analogy for this novel's structure comes only at the expense of another just as important: architecture or, more exactly, cathedral architecture, "frozen music." Proust once called Ruskin's prose (in a review of the French translation of *The Stones of Venice*) a "nef enchantée," an enchanted ship *or* cathedral nave. The repertory of associations—miraculous ark, medieval ship of faith voyaging down the river of Time—he would certainly have wished to appropriate for his own work; and he suggested the cathedral analogy for his *Recherche* more than once. In that metaphor the reader can be thought of as moving through a series of chapels, volume after volume, under the vaulted roof of the whole structure, all the way to the apse and the *adoration perpétuelle* of the Host—or *Time Recaptured*. Letting Scott Moncrieff's "Overture" stand tends to erase one of this novel's metaphorical support systems, just as replacing it with "Narthex" would have erased the other.

The remaining secondary titles, and the overarching Shakespearean tag, have been left as Scott Moncrieff translated them, except that *Albertine disparue* is now *The Fugitive*—Proust's original title, and one that suits a novel based on the truth that *tempus fugit*. The older translations are familiar, and sound right, even though strict accuracy might ask for *Over Toward Swann's Place* for the first volume, and *Toward the Guermanteses'* for the third. The title of volume two actually means something on the order of *In the Shadow of Maidens in Flower,* but in this case Scott Moncrieff kept a firm grip on inaccuracy, settling for *Within a Budding Grove,* and no one has ever blamed him for the discretion.

Albertine's gang of young beauties as "flower maidens"? Marcel never spells out the connection in precise terms; but the smiling bouquets of young women with lofty titles and deep décolletages that he meets on his first evening at the Guermanteses', he compares, with delicate emphasis, to the "filles fleurs" of *Parsifal*. Wagnerian opera, its "endless melody," *Leitmotiven,* and cyclic form helped Proust compose a large-scale human and historical drama, and float it down the symphonic river of Time. (The French word for "saga novel" is *roman-fleuve*.) If we see it as a cathedral, then we might also listen to the *Recherche* as an opera, a Parisian *Parsifal,* with the narrator as an archetypal Pure Fool sent forth on a quest for redemption. Other correspondences: Marcel's madeleine and *tilleul* stand in as a surrogate Eucharist, and we can compare the fateful mother's kiss to the one Kundry bestows on Parsifal to set a seal on those quasimaternal feelings she has for him. The Guermantes milieu, that citadel of titles, riches, and fashion, makes a seductive Klingsor's Castle, with floral sirens as an added enticement to worldliness and sexual entrapment. For the grotesque Klingsor himself, I nominate the Baron de Charlus—though without insisting that any of these correspondences match in every point.

Proust not only reviewed a Ruskin translation but himself translated *The Bible of Amiens;* and he read most of that magnanimous art critic's works, as the scholarly Ruskin essay in *Pastiches et Mélanges* abundantly shows. It's easy to forget that the pre–World War Proust was known as nothing more than worldling, Ruskin translator, and literary critic. He took the risk, formidable for an imaginative writer, of looking like a pedant, aware that this lightened his opponents' task but less concerned to protect himself than to foster truer readings of texts he revered. Proust left brilliant essays on not only Ruskin but also Balzac, Baudelaire, Flaubert, Dostoevsky. If he had never published a novel his essays would still have earned him a place as a critic at least as great as Sainte-Beuve, the "villain" of Proust's anomalous criticism-novel *Contre Sainte-Beuve.* What Proust sought in his sacred texts was the visionary dimension. He opposed "idolatry," the worship of things material and external to the soul. Hence he denied any value to Sainte-Beuve's biographical criticism because it focused on externals and not texts themselves, the most accurate record of spiritual development. He would have lamented those studies of his novel that treat it as a simple roman à clef, the sort that presents, say, Mmede Guermantes as "two parts Comtesse de Greffuhle to three parts Laure de Chevigny," etc.—all of which sounds like some faded recipe for Lady Baltimore cake. Who wants to jingle a bunch of rusty keys when he might simply step inside the cathedral or hear the opera? The metaphysical dimensions to the *Recherche,* the interpretive record of a solitary voyage through life, constitute its real claim on our attention.

The worldly aspect of Proust's novel was nevertheless indispensable, distinguishing it from purely Symbolist works like those of, say, Maeterlinck. Also, the Symbolist dimension likewise distinguishes it from purely realist or naturalist works like Daudet's *Sapho* (a remote ancestor of the *Re-*

membrance) or Zola's *Nana*. Proust had read Ruskin's *The Two Paths* and registered its insistent message that art must include both "tenderness" and "truth." Proust embodies just this bipolar conception in his novel, allotting "tenderness" to childhood, memory, and spiritual aspiration, and "truth" to adulthood, society, and human evil. The two "directions" of this novel, need it be said, correspond to that twofold allotment.

All Proust's commentators note that Swann's and the Guermanteses' directions run as parallel supporting structures throughout the seven volumes; and that the two finally join as one. Swann, the cultivated solitary, of Jewish extraction; the Guermanteses, a highly connected tribe of nobles: what do they epitomize for Proust? One link easy to establish is between the Guermanteses and history, France's chivalric past, with Merovingian barons, Crusaders, Renaissance châtelaines, courtiers at Versailles, and the snobbery of the nineteenth-century Faubourg Saint Germain, consecrated for fiction by Balzac. And Swann? To stroll over toward his place meant taking the *côté de Méséglise,* and, often as not, his direction goes under that designation. In French these syllables are phonetically indistinguishable from the words "mes églises," "my churches." This is the direction of churches, cathedrals even, art works in general, perhaps. But Swann's connoisseurships lean more toward visual art and architecture—the Italian quattrocento, Vermeer, the little churches near Balbec that he recommends to Marcel. (Music one hears in the Faubourg, or at the Opéra, from a box overflowing with jewels and titles.) Then, as Swann's very name implies, he is the exotic, a baptized Catholic, but still by inheritance a Jew, a wanderer, a transient; so that, for example, one goes in the direction of "chez Swann," but toward a demesne inseparable from the Guermantes name. Marcel's travels divide in half as well: to the fashionable hotel at Balbec where he first meets members of the Guermantes clan, and to Venice, the southern city of art with a Romanesque basilica sacred (if by form alone) to Ruskin. If we think of these two as being in the directions Northwest and Southeast with respect to Paris, we have no trouble assigning them to their proper controlling names.

The two metaphoric paths cross and recross throughout the novel and finally prove to belong to one structure, genetically fused at the end in the person of Mlle de St Loup, the daughter of a Guermantes and a Swann. There are many other comparable fusions. Recall the incident of the "steeples of Martinville," in which the young Marcel observes the twin spires of the Martinville church and the single one of Vieuxvicq, during a carriage ride along a winding country road. His shifting vantage point makes the steeples seem to exchange places, and, finally, to line up behind each other into one silhouette. This excursion inspires the boy Marcel's first piece of prose; and the descriptive essay he writes, recast and expanded, eventually appears in the *Figaro* as the adult Marcel's first published work. To him it represented a tentative step toward his vocation; for us it recapitulates the structure of the *Recherche,* a journey along parallel paths that unite at the end.

In *Time Recaptured* the narrator, describing the novel he wants to write, speaks of a "psychology in space" he will have to devise in order to render the multifaceted reality he has come to understand. Characters will be inseparable from the "sites" where they revealed themselves—and establish their identities most firmly in their locations with respect to each other. These relative "positions"—social, familial, sexual—shift time and again throughout the narrative. "Fugitive as the years," this succession of spotlit stages comes by the end to constitute the dimension of Time itself. More than once Proust has been called the Einstein of novel-writing; and his vision of the final unity of Space and Time led him to devise an astonishing novelistic treatment of relativity. My guess is that the earliest glimmering of this insight came not from Einstein but from Wagner. During the first scene change in *Parsifal* Wagner's stage directions keep the curtain up while forest scenery slides away and the two performers on stage are carried aloft on some sort of escalator into the domed hall of the Grail Castle. Just before this transformation, Gurnemanz turns to Parsifal and says, "Du siehst, mein Sohn, zum Raum wird hier die Zeit." In the Universal Theater, Time becomes manifest as a sequence of fast-moving spatial changes. And of course the Swann and Guermantes ways, at their most general, are Space and Time—something implied but hard to discern when, early in the narrative, the two are respectively characterized as "the ideal view over a plain and the ideal river landscape." The reader who wins through to the last page of *Time Recaptured,* however, will know what inferences to draw when the narrator compares old age to standing on "living stilts" made of years and tall as steeples.

Somewhere between painting and music lies literature; but, finally, it seems closer to music. Likewise we think of Proust's subject as Time more than Space and sense that in his hierarchy Vinteuil sat higher than Elstir. Moreover, Time, when recaptured, is the dimension of salvation, while lived time, actual spatial experience, can never, according to Proust, save us—far from it. And the "black gospel" of Proust's pessimism about human love is only one among many repudiations he made in his long assault on idolatry. For Proust, only the achieved soul merits veneration; the rest is dross—riches, social position, even romantic love, even art. That the narrator's *via negativa* actually conceals an optimistic faith becomes apparent only in the last pages of the *Recherche.* When things or places or people are materially absent, when they have been taken away from us, when they exist in no way other than as part of immaterial consciousness, only then do they become sacred. The paradox of involuntary memory points to the central Proustian mystery: how can irretrievably lost moments out of the past return to consciousness as a full, hallucinatory presence? Proust doesn't try to account for the mystery. But it is certainly his surest proof of the immortality of the soul, and presented as such. "The past recaptured" amounts to a trial exercise in redemption, eventually to be repeated at the scale of eternity. If individual consciousness has the power to make vanished times and places present once more, perhaps the soul, after it has entered the long night of death, whether early or late, will be called back involuntarily into universal consciousness by the memory of eternity. Proust wrote as a fool and as a hierophant.

"Men die," said Alkmaion, "because they cannot join the end to the beginning." But just that connection is the task Proust assigned himself. He retreated to a dark chamber (only John Ruskin's self-incarceration at Brantwood during the years of his mental eclipse is comparable), wrote the novel of his life, and let it be the resurrection of his truest and most tender memories. The narrative reaches its conclusion as the hero resolves to write a novel identical in every particular with the novel that his resolution concludes. The end joins the beginning; and no sooner had Proust drafted that inaugural conclusion than he died—and became his readership.

The number of his readers, constantly increasing since Proust's death, will probably multiply exponentially from now on. After all, this novel does come close to being a rare instance of modern scripture, making up in comedy and *savoir mondain* for what it loses in prophetic authority. For most readers certain scenes—the Duchesse de Guermantes's red shoes, the queen of Naples' rescue of Charlus from Mme Verdurin's cruelties, Bergotte's death just after seeing Vermeer's *View of Delft* (to mention three)—immediately take on the clarity and permanence of Platonic forms, part of the available stock of our collective memory, sometimes voluntarily, sometimes involuntarily recalled. If Proust's world was a lost Paradise when his novel appeared fifty years ago, it is doubly so now. All the more sacred then? In any case *The*

Remembrance of Things Past is due to regain its footing after a period of relative neglect; and, whether or not Proust lends his name to the last part of our century, his novel appears ready to come of age, with a new crop of readers, in the fullest and brightest sense.

7

An Anglo-Irish Novelist: Elizabeth Bowen

When Quentin Bell's biography of Virginia Woolf appeared in 1975, the Woolf revival already under way picked up momentum. Victoria Glendinning's *Elizabeth Bowen** probably won't do the same for her. For one thing, Bowen's story lacks the best-seller ingredients Woolf's had—Bohemianism, sexual irregularity, madness, suicide. Beyond that, Glendinning's book, a serviceable, journalistic account, is not so acute as Bell's and much less committed; she seems to doubt the value of her subject. Understandably, Bowen could be described as a disciple of Woolf's, and, since disciples tend to be lesser figures than their masters, Bowen may not be as important as Woolf. She died in 1973 and is still in that limbo the recently deceased are consigned to until critics and the public make up their minds about these writers' historical place and artistic worth. Glendinning merely registers the present uncertainty; she doesn't come down solidly in Bowen's favor—implicitly calling into question the need for this biography.

Glendinning doesn't settle the issue, but at least she poses it, and she has a thesis. She sees Bowen's Anglo-Irish background as the source not just of some of her "material" but of her creativity in general; and "life with the lid on" (Bowen's phrase to describe how she learned in childhood to manage with the personal and domestic confusions facing her) as the

*Alfred A. Knopf, 1978.

dampening influence on that creativity. The first part of the thesis is beyond dispute, unless one ignores Bowen's own statements about the question, and the evidence in her fiction. But, precisely, the Anglo-Irish temperament *includes* the second part. That peculiar temperament emerged as a compound of the local Irish enthusiasm and the imposed English civil and moral order. Installed in large numbers as landowners under the Protectorate, the English stood in roughly the same relationship to the indigenous Catholic population as the superego does to the rest of the mind. But the Irish spirit of place is strong, and succeeding generations were naturally affected by it. Elizabeth Bowen, brought up on lands that had been granted to an ancestor in 1653, came into the conflict as part of her birthright; and it is really intrinsic to her fiction, where all the disturbing forces in psychic life are harnessed to a highly controlled, lucid sense of form. There would hardly be so much control without a need for it; the effect on Bowen's work is not regrettable, but instead beneficent, to judge from those occasional instances where control slips.

If Elizabeth Bowen hadn't left the family seat (an austerely handsome eighteenth-century house named Bowen's Court) she might never have fully developed the English side of her character. Inevitably, she would have been a different writer. She has stated that the Irish don't separate art from artifice, which is arguably better suited to the stage than to the novel—hence Goldsmith, Sheridan, Wilde, Shaw, Beckett, and the others. "Possibly it was England made me a novelist," she says; and for that reason her immigration to England at age seven took on, when she wrote about it in her memoirs much later, a fateful quality.

Elizabeth's father, Henry Bowen, always a "dreamy" man, had a series of nervous collapses beginning when she was six. Finally he had to be committed; whereupon Elizabeth and her mother went to stay with relatives across the Channel. They were passed from hand to hand among sev-

eral towns along the Kentish coast. Elizabeth seemed un-
harmed by this, at least on the surface, but she did develop a
marked stammer about this time and kept it the rest of her
life. In the main, she embraced her new life and its violet
tinge of adventurousness with gusto.

Even so, she never lost touch with Ireland and Bowen's
Court. It was always there to be visited, one of the large
houses to escape burning during the Troubles. Bowen described these Irish country houses as "something between a
raison d'être and a predicament," and the phrase did apply in at
least her case. For her Ireland was a heartland, and she took
up semipermanent residence at Bowen's Court again in the
early 1950s. Eventually living expenses and upkeep forced
Bowen to sell the house in 1959. She believed it was going to
be occupied by the buyer's likable family, but in fact the
property had interested him only because of its timber:
Bowen's Court was torn down. The conjunction of these
facts—home rule, the end of the Anglo-Irish country house
and the Anglo-Irish novel—gives Bowen's life a fabular
character, one a self-styled "romantic" must have reflected
on at length.

The actual discovery of her vocation and molding of her
career took place in London, a series of events displaying a
retrospective plausibility they cannot have had for the Elizabeth Bowen who arrived there in 1918. A national capital
acts as a lodestone to potential artists, conferring its magne-
tism on those capable of being charged with it. Bowen, de-
tecting in herself the instincts of an artist, and having come to
the city where it was possible to be one, at first mistook the
medium: she enrolled in the London County Council School
of Art and tried to paint. This came to nothing. Perhaps she
had assumed her alert eye would naturally bring with it the
gift of rendering visual insights on canvas. An error, but in
her case not tragic—she discovered that the visible world can
be powerfully presented in fiction. By the time Bowen's desire to paint had abandoned her, she'd begun to write stories.

She had also met Rose Macaulay, who recommended the stories to an editor. When they were published, Bowen's ambitions shifted base for good.

Her first collection of short stories, *Encounters,* came out in 1923, and in that same year she married Alan Cameron. The marriage, or perhaps only its never being dissolved before Cameron's death, always puzzled Bowen's friends. A fault of Glendinning's biography is that it doesn't shed much light on Bowen's choice of a husband. The information she does give only makes things more mysterious—the water has been stirred but only muddied. For now, all that's known is that Bowen seems to have accepted to marry Cameron, a fairly ordinary educational administrator, because marriage represented certified adulthood to her, and Cameron was the first suitor to propose to her whom she considered at all "possible." To this Glendinning adds that Cameron had been at Oxford and would have seemed an intellectual to the half-formed, haphazardly educated girl Bowen was. She also mentions that Cameron took his young wife in hand as to the matter of clothes, suggesting that she dispense with some of the unusual jewelry and directing her toward dresses with straight hems and better cuts. This early phase has its comic probability; but why Bowen didn't, after she became one of the most grown-up women of her time, bid farewell to a man for whom she never felt any passion, who found her writer friends dull and was found dull by them in turn, is an unsolved mystery.

Less of a surprise is Bowen's beginning to have affairs outside the marriage, with Cameron's knowledge and fatalistic consent. This habit would have been more acceptable than plodding fidelity, at least among the worldly set of friends that gradually devolved on Bowen as she became known as a novelist. (Some of them she met during her years living at Oxford; others belong to the period of her return to London and taking up residence in a pretty house in Regent's Park.) Even though one or two of the young men she favored seem to have been odd choices, they must have struck friends such as C. M. Bowra and Cyril Connolly as commendable alternatives to the eternal husband. The deepest, most lasting, and probably least objectionable to Bowen's friends was the love affair with Charles Ritchie. He was a Canadian diplomat who came to London just before the war and made himself liked by some of the people Bowen spent time with. In his published diary, *The Siren Years,* Ritchie says, "The first time I saw Elizabeth Bowen I thought she looked more like a bridge-player than a poet," apparently not realizing the categories sometimes overlap. Later, he was to note down after one of Bowen's visits, "I owe her everything." The relationship went on full force all through the war and continued many years afterwards, with some long interruptions, despite Ritchie's marriage in 1948. He was attracted by the family ideal and may also have wanted to establish some sort of logistic symmetry with Bowen's own marriage. For her, divorce never seems to have been a real option. Much about Bowen's relationship with Ritchie will remain conjectural until a more complete biography appears.

Another relationship stinted in this book is Bowen's friendship with Virginia Woolf, whom she met in the early 1930s and saw frequently until Woolf's death in 1941. The friendship was formed and held fast in the face of several dividing factors—generational difference, manner of living, artistic goals. It was bound to be complex, and an understanding of it would almost certainly shed light on the work of both women, since there is an influence relationship between them, possibly even a reciprocal one. The critical problems raised are difficult, and it may be this that caused Glendinning to shy away from a full discussion of Bowen and Woolf. But even aside from the relationship, this biography fails to treat Bowen as a writer, to add to our understanding of her achievement. Since her artistic reputation is still in the balance, no opportunity to discuss her worth should be wasted.

At its peak after the publication of *The Heat of the Day* in 1948, Bowen's reputation began to dim not long after. The angry young men of the 1950s could hardly be expected to care for the work of an implacably good-humored older woman who wrote mostly about the comfortably off and with no more satirical edge than the sort any good novelist always has readily at hand. She was associated with Connolly and the *Horizon* circle; even Connolly at last was forced to acknowledge that it was "closing time in the gardens of the West." The new order looked very much like disorder. Novelists committed to innovation accepted Robbe-Grillet's decree that the nineteenth-century bourgeois novel was dead letter and stopped regarding works of classic fiction like *The House in Paris* or *The Death of the Heart* as models. Bowen herself seems to have noticed a shift in the wind and to have responded to it: her last novel, *Eva Trout,* is very different from the earlier ones. Those who are lukewarm about Bowen in general tend to prefer it to the others; convinced Bowenites like it least. This novel can be praised for having captured some of the harum-scarum quality of life in the jet age, but that comes at a considerable sacrifice of the formal lucidity and sustaining moral vision Bowen was best known for.

As a writer, Bowen must be evaluated on the basis of about a dozen stories and five novels—*The Last September, To the North, The House in Paris, The Death of the Heart,* and *The Heat of the Day.* (A case could be made, too, for *The Little Girls.*). Her nonfiction and autobiographical writings, though they have wit and sometimes genius to recommend them, aren't under consideration here. On the basis of her fiction alone, Bowen is as good as Evelyn Waugh, better than Ivy Compton-Burnett, Graham Greene, or Henry Green. Her novels yield to Woolf's in visionary intensity but are superior to them in formal construction, variety of subject, and moral force.

Bowen is below the greatest novelists—Flaubert, George Eliot, Tolstoy, James, Proust—but like them she reflected constantly and profoundly on the nature of fiction. So much so, that the "laws" of fiction came to constitute a meta-

phorical system for her, used in the novels themselves sometimes to help present the action, as in this passage from *The
Heat of the Day*:

> His concentration on her was made more oppressive by his
> failure to have or let her give him any possible place in the
> human scene. By the rules of fiction, with which life to be
> credible must comply, he was as a character "impossible"—
> each time they met, for instance, he showed no shred or trace
> of having been continuous since they last met.

Conversely, Bowen's brillant "Notes on Writing a Novel"
has a poetic, almost an allegorical quality. She can say, for
example, "Characters must *materialize*—i.e., must have a
palpable, physical reality. . . . Physical personality belongs to
action. . . . Eyes, hands, stature, etc., must appear, and only
appear, *in play*." Discussing dialogue, she says, "Speech is
what the characters *do to each other*." And, in general, "The
presence, and action of the poetic truth is the motive (or mo-
tor) morality of the novel."

It would be wrong, however, to regard Bowen as a
rulebook novelist. The rule she most often waives is the one
proscribing authorial comment. Rather like one of the "inno-
cents" in her own novels, Bowen can't keep quiet about what
she sees and knows. The proportion of comment to narrative
is much higher than Flaubert, say, would have tolerated. Yet
Proust commented even more freely than Bowen, and her
rushes of insight are often as good as his. In both cases you
feel that some principle of genius is at work, so that the propensity must be indulged, and the rules broken—all the more
since the results are so startling. As much by their weaknesses
as by their strengths do artists come into their own.

Part of the moral energy of Bowen's novels resides in just
these passages of authorial comment. In them, she renews for
English fiction the tradition of the French *moralistes*—La
Rochefoucauld, La Bruyère, and the great women diarists
and letter-writers of the eighteenth century. But she is still
squarely within the precincts of fiction: these passages arise

directly from the action presented, and they illuminate what comes after them. Moreover, Bowen isn't deficient in the way many moralists are, so intent on the meaning, purely, of human action they lack sensory awareness. Bowen is all perception. Reading her you realize you have never paid close enough attention to places or persons, the mosaic of detail that composes the first, or the voices and gestures that reveal the second. Her novels invariably take the point of view of an omniscient narrator; and, if *omniscient* means all-seeing as well as all-knowing, the term is especially apt for Bowen. Of course, this very knowingness can be a fault: the reader may feel as though Bowen is always too far ahead, running circles around reader consciousness. This is an unpleasant sensation if only because it gives, inevitably, an impression of unreality: no one feels that life is told by an omniscient narrator; and that point of view in novels is most effective when least obtrusive. For the most part, however, Bowen strikes the right balance between the transparence and opaqueness of reality.

As a prose stylist Bowen is elegant—but quirky. She casts for the short sentence, the clipped epigram. We don't normally associate delicacy of observation with a percussive syntax like Bowen's, but that is her compound. Reading her is like being pelted with feathers, occasionally the quill end. Critics have sometimes complained about her inversions. Habitually she puts the most important word of a sentence in attack position at the beginning or tonic position at the end. By turns, the sentences can seem mannered or forceful. Certainly they contribute to the Anglo-Irish flavor of her writing. Sentences like hers can only be written by someone who has grown up with a special speech-music in the ear.

R. P. Blackmur noted that in Henry James's last novels there was always "a plot which does truly constitute the soul of the action, which does truly imitate the conditions and aspirations of human life as seen in the actions of men and women of more than usual worth and risk." Bowen would certainly have acknowledged these ideals as her own; and she realized them well—except for the last phrase, "more than usual worth and risk." Consistently she made it a part of novelistic plausibility not to invent larger-than-life characters. The figure, so common in her novels, of the innocent young girl forging toward experience leaves an impression less of "worth and risk" than of the destructiveness of innocence, to self and others. Other kinds of characters in Bowen tend to be all too human; we always look a little down at them. Yet if we are in fact experiencing an "ironic" phase in literature, as understood by Northrop Frye, in which fictional characters are typically marginal, hindered, or "low," Bowen can't be called to special account—she is only doing as other moderns do. Larger-than-life characters in modern fiction? There are none; but their absence is felt more keenly in Bowen's novels because in all other ways they exhibit the characteristic strengths of the nineteenth-century classics. The brilliant, humane analysis, the patient, even heroic notation of physical detail, remind us of the older books, and, so conditioned, we scan Bowen's pages with an unconscious expectation of finding heroes there. Their failure to appear, then, disappoints. On the other hand, Bowen has created many magnetic and memorable characters—Stella in *The Heat of the Day,* Emmeline in *To the North,* and (perhaps the nearest Bowen came to inventing a heroic character) the housemaid Matchett in *The Death of the Heart.* All of these go readily into that stock everyone keeps of fictional persons— Mr. Casaubon, Pierre Bezhukov, Mrs. Dalloway, and so forth—characters that have caught special human qualities or attitudes toward experience and come to stand for them. In a fictional world made actual and palpable, Bowen's characters move and make their discoveries, comic or tragic or both together. These novels themselves will soon be rediscovered; new biographical and critical studies would help clarify Bowen's place among English novelists. Weighing real issues, and with a small readjustment of the sights, readers ought to reach a fair view of Elizabeth Bowen—as one of the masters of modern fiction.

III

MELANCHOLY
PASTORALS

8

Fishing by Obstinate Isles:
Five Poets

Charles Tomlinson is not the English poet best known in America: that would probably be Ted Hughes, with Philip Larkin and Thom Gunn coming just after. *Selected Poems 1951–1974,** chosen from eight earlier volumes published between 1951 and 1974, ought to win more readers for Tomlinson; but it isn't likely to compel agreement with one American critic's overheated appraisal of Tomlinson as "the most considerable British poet to have made his way since the Second World War." He is not as good a poet as Larkin or Gunn or Hughes. If marks should be assigned, let him be one of the important English poets, like Geoffrey Hill, who are just now coming into their own, and whose future work may still reorder our sense of their achievement.

Tomlinson displays several characteristics that could be called American (and he probably felt confirmed in these propensities by his reading of Pound): a love of landscape and seascape, and of the act of seeing; a preference for an improvised prosody; a lack of interest in psychology, apart from first-person intuitions; and the choice of vernacular over cultivated speech (the body of locutions based on Latin or neoclassical models). A reader trying to assign some specifically English quality to his poems might find it in their reticence, self-effacement, and tightness. Words, lines, and sentences here give the impression of exaction rather than

---

*Oxford University Press, 1975.

overflow. The careful and unbudgeable phrasing of his se-
curely mortised stanzas can remind us of those immense pre-
Columbian walls in Peru, where hand-hewn monoliths are
wedged together with such precision a knife blade can't be
forced between them. "Stone," in fact, is one of Tomlinson's
rote-words and the subject of many a reflection in his poems.

> All stone. I had passed these last, unwarrantable
>   Symbols of—no; let me define, rather
> The thing they were not, all that we cannot be,
>   By the description, simply of that which merits it:
> Stone. Why must (as it does at each turn)
>   Each day, the mean rob us of patience, distract us
> Before even its opposite?—before stone, which
>   Cut, piled, mortared, is patience's presence.
>   ["On the Hall at Stowe"]

Stone, and after that, water, light, and fire: he is drawn to
what is elemental, and for him the great business of poetry is
sensory perception at its barest, its least tutored. (He has pursued, independently but with no sharp dissociation, an active
career as a painter.) If he has an exceptional eye, his ear is not
far behind; and seeing often converges with hearing in his
poems with memorable results. Here is his rendering of the
night shift at a steel mill:

> There is a principle, a pulse
> in all these molten and metallic contraries,
> this sweat unseen. For men
> facelessly habituated to the glare
> outstare it, guide the girders
> from their high and iron balconies
> and keep the simmering slag-trucks
> feeding heap on heap
> in regular, successive, sea-on-shore
> concussive bursts of dry
> and falling sound.
>   ["Steel"]

"The Chestnut Avenue" might just as fairly be cited, the effects in this case reminiscent of both musical and painterly impressionism:

> Beneath their flames, cities of candelabra
>   Gathering-in a more than civic dark
> Sway between green and gloom,
>   Prepare a way of hushed submergence
> Where the eye descries no human house,
>   But a green trajectory in whose depths
> Glimmers a barrier of stone.

So sensuous, so enthusiastic a poet could never be perfectly at home in the welfare state, and not surprisingly he has written a poem ("More Foreign Cities") thumbing its nose at the prescriptive statement, "Nobody wants any more poems about foreign cities." The poem celebrates travel and even sightseeing, of the right kind. Tomlinson's xenophilia leads him to many happy inventions, including "A Rhenish Winter," "Tramontana at Lerici," and even the trans-Atlantic "Over Brooklyn Bridge." A trip out West, however, produces less good results:

> At the motel desk
> was a photograph of Roy Rogers
> signed. It was here
> he made a stay. He did not
> ride away on Trigger
> through the high night.
>   ["At Barstow"]

Remarking that Tomlinson hasn't evolved much as a poet shouldn't stand in the way of noting his characteristic strengths—exactness, color, music—whether we find them in early poems such as "At Wells" or "Four Kantian Lyrics" or in later ones such as "Clouds," "Appearance," or "After a Death." No more should it prevent singling out an atypical success such as "The Chances of Rhyme," in which this cos-

mopolitan poet retrieves some of the Anglo-Saxon power
sleeping in his language. At a touch, the sleeper awakes:

> The chances of rhyme are like the chances of meeting—
>   In the finding fortuitous, but once found, binding. . . .
>
>   And between
>
> Rest-in-peace and precipice,
>   Inertia and perversion, come the varieties
> Increase, lease, re-lease (in both
>   Senses); and immersion, conversion—of inert
> Mass, that is, into energies to combat confusion.
>   Let rhyme be my conclusion.

If Tomlinson is "American" through his Poundian affinities, by the same token and by the same source John Peck
is a cosmopolitan poet. *Shagbark,* his first book, * made the
debt apparent at surface level: the poems ranged from China
to Europe to America, past and present. Leibniz, Vesalius,
Ch'ien Ku, Kierkegaard, and Maeterlinck had all befriended
Peck, and, it seemed, fortunately. His second book, *The Broken Blockhouse Wall,* † although it points very little to the
great geodesic dome of historical and cultural fact that shel-
ters it, still displays an assured cosmopolitanism at the level
of language and prosody. These verses are finished, elegant,
"advanced," and difficult. Peck is a new American instance
of the durable Symbolist aesthetic, perhaps the only American poet since the early Stevens to draw on Pound as well as
the Mallarmé legacy, with good results.

To call Peck's wily alertness to tradition and lighthanded
relationship to paraphrasable sense in poetry mere sophistica-
tion is to misconstrue him. He intends what he says, and the
accents of sincerity are unmistakable:

*David R. Godine, 1976.
† David R. Godine, 1978.

> and if spasm
> Clicks into place behind
> Your eyes, it is because
> You turn too quickly, you pivot
> Into the trick: the car
> That nearly hits and then
> Shuts you into its speed,
> The night driver whose mirror
> Stripes his eyes, and leaves molten
> The high slope of one cheek
> Charring through: he has yet
> To come, that messenger
> Whom you wish, obscurely, to touch—
> Indifference that survives
> The crossing, the change of suns
> And a cope of stars altered.
>
> ["Lucien"]

Peck's search for special sound effects and rare words meets with mixed success, and readers will alternately prize or consider only precious phrases such as "swirls of steam / Coming off coffee," "Chucking in rubber," "Vaporizes past laughter, toward / The unwit of nowhere," or "Regime of the extreme Scythian / With grip lithic in the mound / Unshatterable in remote permafrost." These studded lines make an undeniable impression. On the other hand, searching for unusual words, what does the poet gain by the new coinage in the lines "To wash secretly / his beshatted drawers," when the perfectly respectable "beshit" already exists? The first condition for originality seems to be an underdeveloped sense of the absurd, and the second, an overdeveloped sense of entitlement.

This book, one can guess, counts most heavily on a middling long sequence called "March Elegies," which takes up a third of the pages. A striking poem by reason of its intricate verbal texture, it can however be read a dozen, two dozen times without its local clarities ever coalescing into any feeling of coherence or verifiability. Though, to be sure, stanzas like the following will register as palpably meaningful:

> The temptation, the believable
> Illusion, is
>   that significance
> Falls into place under one's need like land
>   In its spread fullness.

John Peck has written two books attesting to unusual gifts: he deserves forbearance from the reader, and whatever benefits go with judgment put temporarily aside.

America, the New Golden Land, was settled for venal motives, the thirst for riches, but as well to realize idealistic or pastoral hopes—the recovery of a lost golden age of health, innocence, and pleasure. Characteristic American works of art confront both of these abiding themes, separately or together; but it seems likely that the majority of our novels and poems are versions of pastoral, celebrating unspoiled landscapes and putting complex human issues into simple language. John Hart's *The Climbers** can be inscribed under this rubric, even though his language is not always simple. For him, the human potential must be tested against natural grandeur; placed on the balance with a mountain range, the city is always found wanting. Moreover, Hart conflates the phenomenon of poetry, or perhaps revelation, with the fiercely difficult sport of mountain-climbing, substituting Mount Rainier and its peers for Parnassus. The obvious difference between the two, of course, is that, whereas we climb a mountain just because it's there, a poet writes a poem just because it *isn't* there. Apart from that, mountain-climbers have to face the fact that all available mountains have now been climbed. But not all of Hart's poems take mountain-climbing as their subject.

Hart is a strange poet, temperamentally and stylistically.

---

*University of Pittsburgh Press, 1978.

The frequency of Christian allusion, the odd perceptions jolted into dreamlike dislocations call to mind Robert Lowell—not his *Life Studies,* but the Lowell of the 1940s, surrealist and Catholic.

> Touched the node where six bright vessels bunch,
> snapped the blue stalk of a vein:
> He felt the blood drawn down his wrist
> like a long-stemmed violet fire.
>
> He is dead:
>   The ponderous gem of his skull
> no longer bears his monumental sight.
>   ["Crucifixion"]

At the same time, Hart is a poet capable of drawing the threads of his attention together into luminous transactions with a visible and secular nature:

> The mantis with translucent grin
> climbs up the rack of his six awkward limbs.
>
> So on my palm he settles,
> vein to colder vein,
> stares from a steep face, bony as a stallion's,
> at my enormous focus:
>
> the simple and the chambered eye.
>   ["Confrontation"]

In a poem called "Flying into Los Angeles" Hart is stung into beshrewing the fallen culture that has produced such infernal habitations; the malediction goes beyond the unruffled pastoral disdain of cities and well into the jeremiads of Old Testament prophecy. Unfortunately the language of prophecy is ill sorted with the flat actualities of jet travel and modern urban sprawl, and, however justly provoked the author, the poem sinks under its own weight. (Besides: surely Lucifer has worked greater mischief than the city of Los Angeles.)

These caveats are not meant to deny that Hart has an authentic gift. For one thing, he shows more than amateur skill in handling traditional meter and rhyme, surely the most daring approach to poetic form nowadays. How many other young poets can write convincing rhymed tetrameter couplets or poems in terza rima? This is clearly an independent spirit, and to be encouraged. In any case, it takes no special indulgence to read and appreciate Hart's "Elaboration on a Line from the *Mandaean Liturgies*," an arresting new treatment of an old dilemma: whether Gnostic beliefs can be harmonized with the adept's inescapable love for "Tibil," the fallen earthly realm.

> The col is bright where Adam stood
>
> to start the errors of the climb
> and we have uses yet for time
>
> and beg of you the gentleness
> to leave the climbers in distress.

Czeslaw Milosz's poems, translated from Polish by the poet and Lillian Vallee and collected in *Bells in Winter,* * give the impression that they have been brought to completion against overwhelming odds. Historical, biographical, and temperamental forces militated against their being written. To have grown up within a rich native tradition and then have one's home shattered by war and one's political hopes disappointed; to have lost one's country and emigrated to another, with its own style of disappointment: as much as these events might provide subjects for poems, they might also take away the desire to write at all, poetry in this case a *casualty* of imposed cosmopolitanism. Milosz must be applauded

*The Ecco Press, 1979.

for having managed to write his poems, and with honorable results.

No translation ever conveys much of the real poetic power of the original. The poems translated here sound like English, which is in itself a notable achievement. The pity is that they cannot sound like Polish; therefore no decisive conclusions can be reached by the present writer about the poems as verbal artifacts. Perhaps this is less of a drawback with Milosz than it might be with others. He says, for example, "(I have always lacked words and have not been a poet / If a poet is supposed to take pleasure in words)." And again:

What I'm saying here is not, I agree, poetry,
as poems should be written rarely and reluctantly,
under unbearable duress and only with the hope
that good spirits, not evil ones, choose us for their instruments.

["Ars Poetica"]

Yet it is suffering and righteous anger that most often inspire Milosz to write. One can infer that he is drawn to a saintly ideal, ascetic, perhaps Gnostic: "Who can tell what purpose is served by destinies / And whether to have lived on earth means little or much." And then:

Do you remember your textbook of Church History?
Even the color of the page, the scent of the corridors.
Indeed, quite early you were a gnostic, a Marcionite,
A secret taster of Manichean poisons
From our bright homeland cast down to the earth,
Prisoners delivered to the ruin of our flesh
Unto the Archon of Darkness. His is the house and law.

These passages are drawn from a long poem in six parts titled "From the Rising of the Sun." It's a magisterial work, a summing up of a life at moments grateful and at others agonized. As a whole it constitutes the poet's testament of despair and hope against hope. In the absence of any evidence, he still believes in *apokatastasis,* or restitution: "For me, therefore, everything has a double existence. / Both in time and when time shall be no more." Living in the heart of paradox the poet imagines the coming of the millennium, when:

The demiurge's workshop will suddenly be stilled. Unimaginable
  silence.
And the form of every single grain will be restored in glory.
I was judged for my despair because I was unable to understand
  this.

The last sentence should not be accepted at face value. The poet has suffered, meditated, and written. The task of understanding is not finally his alone.

*Hello, Darkness** includes the three volumes of poetry L. E. Sissman published while he was alive—*Dying: An Introduction* (1968), *Scattered Returns* (1969), and *Pursuit of Honor* (1971)—and adds to these thirty-nine poems written after the last collection. Except for juvenilia and occasional pieces, here then is all of Sissman's poetry, as his editor Peter Davison states in a sympathetic and crisply written memoir prefacing the volume.

Sissman's poetry, like his life, is singular and problematic. Possibly a good many Harvard graduates now executives in advertising agencies write verse; some may have published it; one or two may, like Sissman, have discovered themselves stricken with a fatal illness (in his case, Hodgkin's disease). But surely no one else, after such knowledge, could then go on to write a poem in which a biopsy specimen (it "Turns out to end in -oma") is described as "my / Tissue of fabrications." Nearly all of Sissman's poems were written after the discovery, and nearly all of them are, at least by moments, funny, sometimes outrageously so. How is this to be accounted for? Auden said that wit demanded imagination, moral courage, and unhappiness: "an unimaginative or a

*The Atlantic Monthly–Little, Brown, 1978.

cowardly or a happy person is seldom very amusing." Sissman is a witty and amusing poet indeed; and he must have
fulfilled the conditions mentioned. But the laughter afforded
by these poems—once the reader *knows*—is of a peculiar
kind; it is as hard to hold as dry ice; it chills, it burns, and
vanishes in white smoke.

Without the resources of wit, irony, and moral detachment
a writer cannot successfully treat the subjects that attracted
Sissman. A poem titled "A College Room: Lowell R-34"
will hardly be written with an entirely sober mien, any more
than one titled "Lüchow's and After." You must go to Sissman if you want to hear a treatment in verse of subjects such
as undergraduate days at Harvard in the 1940s, or the life of a
successful businessman shuttling back and forth between
Boston and New York, or the preoccupations and habits of
the upper middle classes, their marriages, families, and
dalliances outside these. Sissman's "true Penelope was
Flaubert," one is tempted to say; but even in prose fiction
these matters have seldom been observed and noted with
comparable attention to detail. Like the late John O'Hara,
Sissman knows which Gotham restaurants, bars, and hotel
lobbies are likely to yield promising subjects, which character wears the Meledandri shirt, which the Peck & Peck
frock, and which the thick-soled Jarman shoe. To this arcane
body of knowledge he adds the general stock of culture most
poets draw on, and his readiness to slap down the credit card
of literary allusion suggests he assumes someone else is pick-
ing up the tab. In a quite serious poem, "On the Island,"
Sissman styles the drive out to Sag Harbor as "Starting for
Paumanok"; and in "At the Bar, 1948," he sums up a tryst
thus:

> In this sub-basement of
> The Tower of Babel, full of talk of love
> Which glances off our faces, we conclude
> Our business over stingers, each betrayed

> By an embezzling partner. In whose bed
> Did we commit each other's substance to
> A voided contract, countersigned with no
> Co-maker's name? No matter. In this place
> Of love and excrement, only the face
> Of one's true love is legal tender.

The passage points to other Sissmanian earmarks—his punning and extended conceits. Verbal play is of course "popular," even vulgar, and it has never suited refined writers, from Gibbon to Cyril Connolly, who couldn't be expected to give a word-for-word endorsement of the works of Shakespeare or James Joyce. But Sissman doesn't mind that his verses have lapses of taste; he doesn't insist that they lead sheltered lives. The puns are left in, along with other kinds of wildly proliferating wit—temporary ambiguities set up by enjambment, wrenched Byronic rhymes, parodies, and ingenious solving of prosodic problems. The poems remind us that ingenuity is one of the forms the irrational takes in poetry (as the root *genius* suggests) and that it is a kind of divination. The poet who works out a conceit, for example, soon has to break through the normal condition of self-deception and tell everything he knows in order that all possible analogies between reality and its metaphors be drawn. The conscious desire to be artful seduces the unconscious into yielding up what it has been hoarding. Skill is a *daimon*, part and parcel of

> the serious business of what
> An artist is to do with his rucksack
> Of gift, the deadweight that deforms his back
> And drives him on to prodigies of thought
> And anguishes of execution.

At the same time it should be remarked that Sissman can dispense with these tools and still produce excellent lines, as in this memento mori:

> Tonight, though, it is almost worth the price—
> High stakes, and the veiled dealer vends bad cards—
> To see the moon so silver going west,
> So ladily serene because so dead,
> So closely tailed by her consort of stars,
> So far above the feverish, shivering
> Nightwatchman pressed against the falling glass.
>   ["December 27, 1966"]

What is strange is that the horrifying hospital poems near the end of *Hello, Darkness* do rely on Sissman's usual wit and detachment; the voice coming, for most intents, from beyond the grave keeps its humor in the presence of the unforgivable. The pain and ignominy of illness are given clearance to become the substance of the poems "Clotho: A Hospital Suite" and "Cancer: A Dream," poems the more unbearable to read as the poet's patience is exemplary. It is well that the volume concludes not with these but with the remarkable "Tras Os Montes," an unflinching and sovereign gesture toward the imagined landscape of death:

> where self,
> Propelled by its last rays, sways in the sway
> Of the last grasses and falls headlong in
> The darkness of the dust it is part of
> Upon the passes where we are no more:
> Where the recirculating shaft goes home
> Into the breast that armed it for the air,
> And, as we must expect, the art that there
> Turned our lone hand into imperial Rome
> Reverts to earth and its inveterate love
> For the inanimate and its return.

9

Cavafy and Alexandrianism

I first heard of Cavafy in a footnote: the "old poet of the city" invoked in the opening of Lawrence Durrell's *Justine*. Including a translation of Cavafy's "The City" was Durrell's way of acknowledging a debt and hinting at one of the conceptual cornerstones of his labyrinthine tetralogy. When I read it, I was a college student without much travel experience. Alexandria I knew of as one of Eliot's Unreal Cities, otherwise, a dot on a map. Durrell's incantatory "Five races, five languages . . . more than five sexes, and only de-motic Greek seems to distinguish among them" worked as a heady incentive to get to know foreign tongues. To date, I have only learned three, demotic Greek not one of them, nor even *katharevousa* (the written idiom used in old-fashioned belles lettres and in daily newspapers). I haven't been to Egypt yet and notice that those who go seldom make a de-tour to visit the mere geographical site of a city that, in a sense, is no longer there. Cavafy's Alexandria glimmers, for me, behind a threefold veil of language, space, and time. To grasp it I have to depend on intermediaries and the sympathetic imagination.

The Dalven and Keeley-Sherrard translations have at least left ajar the door into Cavafy's rooms on the rue Lepsius, their walls, windows, and long perspectives onto the decline and extinction of Hellenism in the southern Mediterranean. Cavafy's subject evolved slowly. After some early poems on Homeric themes, written in the 1890s, he gradually drew into focus his most congenial matter, the art, moral reflections, religious aspiration, and earthly passions of a few dozen

Ptolemaic Alexandrians. That Antioch in Syria was brought into this poetic ambit, as well as several other cities in Asia Minor (Constantinople as late as the twelfth century), points to a central Cavafian insight: the peculiar configuration of spirit he had singled out in Hellenistic Alexandria can be found in many different places and times. Actually, some of the poems take place "in the present," an Alexandria defined only by subject matter and tone, never by name.

George Seferis in an essay on Cavafy and Eliot singles out the sense of the past as a characteristic these two poets share. But there are other more striking resemblances. The past summoned by both poets serves to frame a present pervaded by regret, an awareness of cultural debility, and an abashed sexuality. Mere coincidence? It may be that Eliot knew of Cavafy, even before he wrote *The Waste Land*. Eliot would almost certainly have read E. M. Forster's Alexandrian essays, first published in *The Athenaeum* in 1919 and later collected in *Pharos and Pharillon,* in which Forster describes Cavafy and his poetry. Without these essays, would Eliot have thought to include neglible Alexandria in his catalogue of falling capital cities? And would he have invented "Mr. Eugenides, the Smyrna merchant," who invites Eliot's narrator to the louche Cannon Street Hotel, a narrator who identifies himself in the next verse paragraph as "Tiresias"? At least one other reader seems to have noted this convergence. Robert Liddell, Cavafy's biographer in English, once wrote an Alexandrian novel called *Unreal City*. Among Liddell's cast of characters is one based on Cavafy; his name is Christos Eugenides. Alexandria and Alexandrians are whenever and wherever you find them.

The particular way in which Alexandria is unreal and unlocal arises from its situation in a certain place and in a certain history. It was always a watery kingdom—the Venice of Africa, perhaps. Founded on the Canopic mouth of the Nile, and with a conveniently wide harbor, it was one of the greatest ports of the Mediterranean, a conduit for the immensely lucrative Egyptian grain and, later, cotton trades. Just south lay the brackish waters of Lake Mareotis, which is still there; but the Nile waterway silted up centuries ago. In a land celebrated for the preservation of physical remains over the millennia, this one city stands out as surprisingly careless of its real estate. The glorious city of the Ptolemies has vanished entirely, leaving nothing behind but the record, and even that fragmentary. Christians and then Moslems burned the contents of the legendary library. The wonder-of-the-world lighthouse was destroyed and its stones dispersed. Londoners and New Yorkers, for a while, thought they had received one of the last extant pieces of Antony's and Cleopatra's tomb when, in 1878, the Khedive sent to them obelisks billed as "Cleopatra's Needles." They are still standing on the Embankment in London and near the Metropolitan Museum in New York. But they have nothing to do with Cleopatra. Octavian brought them to Alexandria from Heliopolis around 9 B.C., where they rested until nineteenth-century Egyptian public relations found another use for them. It is true that some of present-day Alexandria's street plan dates back to the Ptolemies; for example, the rue Rosette, where Cavafy lived for many years, was once the great Canopic Way, with the Gate of the Sun and Gate of the Moon at opposite ends. But all the ancient structures have been demolished and even their ruins have vanished.

The Alexandrian propensity to crumble and dissolve is used by Shakespeare in fashioning his own Ptolemaic myth. "Let Rome in Tiber melt," Antony's first tirade begins, but it is pronounced far from Rome. Antony has been losing the dryness of the Roman-Republican temper under the dissolving genius of Hellenistic Egypt, which may be figured as Cleopatra bearing a cup of wine. It is as Venus Born-of-the-Foam that she first appears to him, draped fluidly on a couch in her river barge. In no time these new avatars of Venus and Bacchus are jointly ruling Cleopatra's sumptuous corner of the Delta. As the scenes quickly tumble over each other, the fatal sea battle at Actium is engaged and lost—whereas Antony's troops swear to him they could have won any battle

on land. "Authority melts from me," Antony mourns as his
subordinates desert. The dissolving process is well along; or,
in Shakespeare's coinage, things "discandy." Menaced with
captivity and public humiliation in Rome, Cleopatra would
first "melt Egypt into Nile" and see herself stretched out
naked on the Nilotic mud that breeds "aspics." Underlying
all these dissolutions is the old tradition that tells how
Cleopatra dropped a pearl into wine (or vinegar) and let it
melt. "My draught to Antony shall far exceed it," she said as
she swallowed the potion. Shakespeare neither dramatizes
nor even alludes to this scene, perhaps because it too closely
resembled one he had already written. In the last scene of
Hamlet a poisoned pearl (or "union") dropped into a cup of
wine kills Gertrude and Claudius. The reunion permitted to
Antony and Cleopatra and to the royal Danes is the one provided by death, the severed connection to material life.
Hamlet seems to have anticipated from his first entrance this
releasing good-bye to earthly existence. He says, "Oh, that
this too, too solid flesh would melt, / Then, and resolve itself
into a dew."

Cavafy saw a trace of Alexandria in Shakespearean Den-
mark. His poem "King Claudius" recounts the terrible
events of the play after the fact and from the point of view of
a nameless peasant loyal to Claudius. This shift of vantage
allows for a rich deployment of ironic perspectives. It is Cavafian to find in the pleasure-loving usurper something more
engaging even than the moral torments of a wronged prince.
As for *Antony and Cleopatra,* Cavafy's poem "The God Abandons Antony" has something to add to the dramatist's portrayal of his royal renegade. When the god's withdrawal is
mentioned in the play, we are told that Hercules, himself
born a mortal, has abandoned Antony. In the poem, the god
whose "invisible procession" departs "with exquisite music"
is not Hercules but Alexandria itself.

There are many precedents for the deification of mortals in
classical tradition. A Roman emperor ready to assume divine
status could invoke the mythological example of Hercules or

even the historical Alexander. Alexander's unexpected eleva-
tion took place only after he had founded his namesake city.
When Alexander came out into the desert to meet him, the
oracle-priest Ammonis called the hero "Son of God," and the
designation was not refused. Alexander's imperial Roman
successors could embody the mythological weight of such a
title as conveniently as he: the nearer empire comes to theocracy, the more stable it is likely to be. Cities themselves
were never worshiped as gods—though of course there were
cities *of* God, the Jerusalem that the faithful do not forget,
and Rome of the Holy Church that foreshadows that other
heavenly Rome. Cavafy boldly apotheosizes Alexandria itself—even as this deity is withdrawing from its failing ad-
herent. If Cavafy is one of the great poets of memory, that is
partly because his divine city, too, so well epitomizes muta-
bility and the spiritual activity that comes to replace material
presence and power. "Fallings away, vanishings": even fairly
recent history continues to strike this note. When he was de-
posed in 1952, King Farouk chose to depart (and begin his
own Antony's exile) from the port of Alexandria.

In the fluctuant city, boundaries shift, things rise and just
as precipitately fall. A god descends to fraternize with mortals, and a few of these become divinities. Disparate religions
peacefully coexist and often crossbreed. The cult of Serapis,
for example, was founded as late as the Ptolemaic period.
This Hellenic deity was formed on an Egyptian prototype,
itself a fusion of the attributes of Apis, the Memphian bull,
and Osiris, Lord of the Dead. By assimilating him to the
Greek Hades and representing him in an anthropomorphic
statue, the new dynasty symbolically united Europe and Africa and confirmed its divine legitimacy. But the Ptolemies
were open to other religious currents as well. From the beginning there was an important colony of Jews in Alexandria, and in the third century B.C., according to tradition,
Philadelphus commissioned a Greek translation of Hebrew
scripture, which came to be known as the Septuagint. Not
until the first century B.C. was the task of translation com-

pleted. Indispensable to the Alexandrian Jews, who no longer read Hebrew, it also made Judaic tradition available to the Hellenistic world for the first time and assisted in the conversion of a growing number of Gentiles drawn to Jewish religion.

By the same token, the Septuagint was a prime instrument in the development of Christian theology and proselytization among both Jews and pagans. And in the long battle to achieve a coherent Christian orthodoxy, Alexandrians were among the chief contestants. The Arian heresy, for example, Hellenistic in its insistence on the humanity of Jesus, was born in North Africa, only to be countered later by Athanasius and the creed that is still in use. (Athanasian orthodoxy, however, fared better in all the *other* cities of Christendom. The Alexandrian faithful either followed the Coptic tradition, grounded in the Monophysite heresy, or, eventually, severed ties with Rome in favor of the patriarch of Constantinople.) If religion in Alexandria was made to submit to the scrutiny of Hellenistic philosophy, the reverse may also be said. Alexandrian thinkers wrote in an aspirational mode, especially Plotinus, whose mystic extension of Platonism influenced schoolmen and poets for more than a thousand years after his death.

The Alexandrian ferment and blur of religious thought gave Cavafy substance for many of his poems. Several, for example, portray the career of that notorious backslider, Julian the Apostate. Universal scorn greeted Julian's abandonment of Christianity in favor of the old pagan deities, for he tried to promulgate a puritan strain of Neoplatonism no more acceptable to the Philhellenes than to the Christians. The poem "Julian at the Mysteries" allows Cavafy to have fun at everyone's expense. When the apostate sees shadowy figures (ostensibly the spirits of the Olympian gods), his terror makes him forget that he is no longer Christian: he crosses himself. The figures vanish, leaving Julian shaken and doubtful. Has the Cross then been more powerful than these spirits? A priest dismisses Julian's surmise, saying that the

gods had simply found his gesture too vulgar to put up with
and had departed. A final layer of irony is added when the
poem concludes with these words:

> This is what they said to him, and the fool
> recovered from his holy, blessed fear,
> convinced by the unholy words of the Greeks.

This conclusion reveals the poem as a characterized monologue, spoken by an unidentified Christian coeval of Julian's.
Cavafy's point is not to say who was "right" but simply to
give the reader a kaleidoscopic portrayal of religious con-
tention in a transitional age, and always with a nimbus of
subtle comedy. Something similar was attempted later in
Forster's *A Passage to India*. It takes a special angle of vision to
discover in credal conflict—one of the saddest themes in history—not merely ignorance and tartuffery but instead a spiritual deadlock that both dismays and bemuses.

The price of admission to the Cavafian mysteries is high.
Even with more than usual preparation, anybody, I assume,
is grateful for an annotated edition of the poems. The Alexandrian tradition was always, to be sure, a learned one,
knowing it could rely on an audience accustomed to reading
the classics. That the intensely civilized Alexandrian Theocritus should have invented *pastoral* poetry can really surprise no one aware of the handsome rusticity of the Katsura
palace, or the vogue for Rousseau among late eighteenth-
century French aristocrats, or present-day American cos-
mopolites' liking for the states of Maine or Vermont. Cavafy
himself is pastoral only in an expanded Empsonian mode. He
has no landscapes; but he peoples his poems with rough
equivalents to Theocritus's simple-hearted swains. Pastoral
simplicity in these poems of latter-day Alexandria is one with
their immediacy. No historical or literary lore is required to
follow them, as in most of Cavafy. They surely helped Cavafy find a following faster than the more complex historical
pieces would have.

How much of Cavafy's early popularity can be accounted for by the "anomalous" or "illicit" nature of the passions recounted in these poems? (I assume the Greek for these words that appear so often in Cavafy is less musty.) No other poet of the time was then publishing poems about love between men; in fact, love poetry of any sort, except for album verse, was as scarce then as now. Cavafy's poetry could be enjoyed and recognized as excellent by many readers secure in their own sexual preference even when it differed from his. On the other hand, some discriminating tastes—Marguerite Yourcenar, Kimon Friar—judge that the love poems are marred by sentimentality. For that defect there are only subjective yardsticks. And perhaps the effect of whatever sentimentality one finds in the poems can be tempered by reflecting on the courage that was required to write them when Cavafy did. I wonder, too, whether the very Alexandrian *Mémoires d'Hadrien* could have been written without the precedent Cavafy set. Why, for that matter, did Cavafy himself never think to write about at least Antinoüs (assuming that the all too Roman Hadrian failed to engage his imagination)? The visit of the imperial pair to Alexandria with its open allusion to Alexander and the young Hephestion (whose tomb was still prominent there), Antinoüs's watery death in the Nile, all of that should have served brilliantly. But then Yourcenar's Egyptian chapters, written in a prose close to poetry, can perhaps substitute for what Cavafy might have done.

More celebrated in his time even than Theocritus was Callimachus, who set the tone for the Alexandrian school. "A big book [i.e., long poem] is a big bore," he said (a battle cry raised some two thousand years later by Edgar Allan Poe). Callimachus would allow only short, highly finished lyrics, novel in meter, form, and sensibility. Cavafy holds to that standard. His longest poem is just under a hundred lines, and most hover around sonnet length. As to form, Cavafy was innovative for his time: he uses irregular line lengths, variable meter, and sporadic rhyme. In a more essential sense, the originality of the poems resides in what they dispense with. Cavafy despised the rhetorical bombast of the Athens school of his day; he writes with almost no heightening at all. Metaphors are absent except as speech idioms. The only figure much used is anaphora (the repetition of a connective word or phrase), which lends an incantatory tone to these largely declarative poems. Cavafy's language is a subtle mixture of demotic and *katharevousa*—it is "tainted with purist," as Kimon Friar has said. The reader with no modern Greek can get some idea of the lexical sensation produced by looking at Auden's poems of the late thirties and early forties, where slang and archaism strike sparks off each other. And Cavafy made sure to stamp his verse with local watermarks by using locutions indigenous to Alexandria.

In "The First Step" (1899), a young poet complains to Theocritus of his slow progress: two years and he has managed only one idyll. Theocritus reproves him and points out that this first step already sets the youth apart from the mass of men. He is now enrolled in the "city of ideas," a hard and unusual achievement. This notion of poetic citizenship, a sort of declaration of intent for the young Cavafy, should be adduced for a fuller reading of the pivotal 1910 poem, "The City." Here the narrator addresses himself as "you" and complains of the sense of entrapment and stagnation he feels having spent so many years in the same narrow ambit—it's time he found a better city to live in. The second paragraph demolishes this proposal:

This city will always pursue you. . . .
Don't hope for things elsewhere;
there's no ship for you, there's no road.
Now that you've wasted your life here, in this small corner,
you've destroyed it everywhere in the world.

If Cavafy never names Alexandria in the poem, it is only to make sure that we recognize the symbolic resonances. He means not only the provincial backwater in northern Africa but also the mythic City of Ideas, of poetry, and, more particularly, of Alexandrianism in poetry. He will discover this anomalous, separate reality wherever he goes; Alexandria and Alexandrians are wherever and whenever one finds them. The divine status conferred on the city is both a creation and fate. After 1910, Cavafy came to experience this interior myth as a form of freedom. He ceases being preoccupied with the walls of the rue Lepsius apartment and goes out into the streets of his city to take in its perspectives on the past and the present.

Cavafy's Alexandria joins that peculiarly modern tradition of the mythicized city—Baudelaire's Paris, Whitman's Mannahattan, Proust's Venice, Joyce's Dublin, Eliot's London, Williams's Paterson—and is far from the least of these. Indeed the calm disillusionment, the ironic perceptiveness, and the dissolute, faintly seedy atmosphere of Cavafy's city has become one of the touchstones of the modern sensibility. Directly or indirectly it affected not only Durrell but surely Beckett, Burroughs, Pynchon, and even the quizzical narrator of Camus's *La Chute,* who is as much at home in the "Bar Mexico City" in Amsterdam as ever Cavafy was in the Café Khédivial. Of the writers who have read him closely, how many will be willing to draw up a complete inventory of the debt?

To call Cavafy disillusioned or *désabusé* needs qualifying. Daily confronted with an undermining lucidity, he is more than ready to embrace illusion—insofar as a conscious decision to do so allows illusion to operate. His poems in that mode give off the air of having enchanted the author at least as long as their music lasted. Yet, when an inevitable lifting of the veil comes, there are no signs of agony. Instead, a lofty, paradoxical gleam comes into the lines, the tone of *I knew this all the while.* For the aristocratic artist, a certain near-omniscience figures as a pleasure not surpassable—no matter how changed and fallen the resulting personal condition appears in the flickering light of knowledge.

I like to think of Cavafy as he is portrayed in the final photograph of 1932, long after he considered himself to have
aged into an inadmissible, un-Hellenic *laideur*. The man who
stops to observe and condemn his looks can never, of course,
fully accept the verdict. Those with ordinary plainness—the
greatest number, after all—rather like the way they look and
do not judge. It requires narcissism to love or hate the image
in the mirror. But this narcissism can take the form of a de-
fiant vaunting of unbeauteous features before a crude and un-
deserving world as often as it leads to anxious efforts at
cosmetic improvement. Cavafy seems to have trod a middle
path, done what he could about the baldness and so on, but
let his face be the timeworn *kosmos* it was to all onlookers.
And surely his judgment was too harsh, unless beauty
amounts to no more than symmetrical features and a golden
tan. The photograph shows that Cavafy's was a Greek face,
proud, effortlessly serious, battered and grooved into perfect
legibility. The eyes, from having looked at so many lives and
so many ages, are wary, stoic, beyond the melodrama of despair. They gaze elsewhere, not at us. And yet it is hard not
to imagine he wouldn't respond if jogged out of his daydream by the right words from the flock of his younger disciples. He had surely read Callimachus's *Aition*, one passage of
which says, "That old man ages with a lighter heart, whom
young men hold in affection, and whom they lead up to his
door by the hand, like one of their own elder kin."

Melancholy Pastorals: George Barker and Robert Pinsky

In a world that is becoming ever more precisely quantifiable, and where that precision has the force of fatality, art functions as a sort of wild card in the deck. All other institutions must be able to state their formal identities and establish credit; but art remains, finally, unaccountable, and that is one of its chief virtues. We might consider music or painting to be the least determinate among the arts, but verbal fictions, poems, share in that indeterminacy. They do so partly because *all* forms of discourse involve a degree of ambiguity, partly because of the vexed philosophical status of statements made in verbal fictions, and partly because convention freely allows for unrationalized, unconventionalized, even anarchic impulses in poems. We can never quite pin down a poem, and that allows us to go on talking about it for decades, for centuries—whereas nothing stops conversation as fast as a statistic. Poems permit us, in short, to bring our own anarchy to bear on a discussion that can never be altogether rationalized. The process is strangely energizing, and so we generally view the indeterminate, anarchic aspects of art as a manifestation and as a sustainer of vitality.

Confronted with actual instances, however, our commitment to the anarchic in poetry may weaken. My feelings about the poetry of George Barker divide on just this issue. On one side, a tonic satisfaction from contemplating the grand original, all-or-nothing poet he has tried to be—often, we may guess, at the expense of his own personal happiness. On the other, actual readings of the poems, where words in sequence, and not biographies or poetic manifestoes, are what must be responded to. Barker writes *extreme* poems; as though bad taste carried as far as possible might be a form of the sublime.

The jacket to *Villa Stellar** has this note about the book by its author: "It has two purposes. The first to record biographical instances and the second to record the frames of mind in which these incidents and instances were recollected. I have tried to describe the changing colours of the memory, as the dolphin might, if it could, try to describe the altering colours of its skin as it dies." This comment didn't quite stop me from opening the book, where is to be found an opening dedicatory poem, "Written at the Waterfall of Vyrnwy," and a sequence of untitled lyrics numbered I to LVIII, each less than a page long. The sequence is set in Italy—Rome, Lake Albano, Lerici, Apulia, and (perhaps only in reverie) the source of the Clitumnus, familiar to readers of Vergilian pastoral. About half of the poems are meditations, the rest, at least minimally, narratives. Three other characters figure in the sequence (apart from the narrator): a "Contessa," a painter called Kingsmill, and a woman (possibly Scottish) called Elizabeth Roberta Cameron. The exact relationships among the four are never defined, but to call them friends will do.

The poetic meditations (Barker's "frames of mind") are devoted to the great subjects—eros, death, art, the past, drink, suffering, madness—that have obsessed Barker since the publication of his first book, in 1933. To add some perspective here, it may help to summarize his development as a poet. His has been an uncharacteristic career, without the usual university associations. Instead, multiple apprenticeships: to Pound; to the avowed Surrealist David Gas-

*Faber & Faber, 1979.

coyne; to (this part is usual enough) T. S. Eliot, whom he met when he was twenty; and for a time to Auden and his group. He published in a few numbers of *The Left Review,* but the linkage was unstable. He later summed up this leftist phase with the admission that he had once "entertained the Marxian whore." More congenial were the writers of the self-styled New Apocalypse—Henry Treece, J. F. Hendry, G. S. Fraser, others. *The White Horseman* (1941) published by this circle advocated anarchism and exalted the individual as asocial, Freudian, myth-ravaged, Orphic. It is in the climate of British 1940s Romanticism that Barker seems least anomalous. If we can reconstruct the temper of the years of the long Yeatsian afterglow, when Dylan Thomas was at his peak, and when Alex Comfort and Anne Ridler were publishing steadily, then Barker's poetry will seem very plausible.

Still, when section XXII of *Villa Stellar* asks the question,

Can the heart ever return to the house of its origin where
a window looked out onto that prospect of fields and flowers,
     always
it seemed patterned in the harlequin tints of
early childhood? And where a conjuring stream transformed a dead dog into Hermes with wings and stars?

the answer must clearly be no. Nor will many disagree with the Contessa when, in section XLIX, she says:

I am sick of the bouquets
of broken mirrors and barbed wire and rubber bladders
     containing
specimens of someone else's intellectual urine
mitigated, if one is lucky, by only the faintest odour
of a self abjuring its pity. I am quite sick of
the honesty that insists upon regurgitating into my lap
simply because I am sitting here.

This is Barker at his most masochistic—a lover's quarrel with the self, no doubt. But, titters aside, fairness demands that these poems be given their due; the Contessa (or Barker) has not really described his poems, or not all of them. Barker has also written novels, and some of the most persuasive sections in *Villa Stellar* resemble bite-sized short stories—funny, in the manner of V. S. Pritchett, grotesque, like Iris Murdoch.

> So the Contessa invited us to attend a piano recital
> in the music room at the villa. Kingsmill refused and
> Elizabeth Roberta Cameron put on her Wellington boots,
> masked her enormous eyes in goggles of mascara and
> we traipsed rather moodily up the garden path to
> sprinkling Chopin. A bald young German maestro
> milked the Steinway, and the Cameron sat nibbling at
> a large bowl of macaroons. I observed that she had
> removed one of her Wellingtons and surreptitiously
> scratched away at her instep as with her other hand she
> fished for more biscuits. She leaned over and whispered:
> "Very soon you will have to excuse me. I am
> utterly tone deaf to all instruments except the bagpipes."
> We got up and left. She sneaked a few macaroons
> as she rose from her chair. The young German pianist
> played us back down the garden path with another exquisite
>   Prelude.

This section (XVII) is prosy, but most are not. One of the strategies of the book is constantly to vary the tone, the substance, the metric format, as a way to keep the reader engaged. Almost all of the poems use meter, but the long lines are subtly varied; and some periodic forms, with rhymes, are brought in occasionally, even one irregular sonnet. There is never any doubt that, in addition to telegrams from the unconscious, the poem is informed by conscious art.

Barker can write striking and perhaps memorable phrases. He speaks, for example, of "the first livid gleam / of the cut-glass moon as she enters, the dying Diana / when the wine bottle shines with its mirage of instant solutions. . . ." He demonstrates that rare ability to *image* concepts, to find objective correlatives for thought: "Love is the fact of its object. Without it nothing can enter / the sanctum sanctorum of our subjective perceptions / like the hole in the dome of the Pantheon for the god to descend through." He describes moral codes as "wholly artificial systems we have constructed to protect ourselves," and says they "function / like St Paul's dark glasses, to prevent our being blinded." This metaphoric mode is much more successful than the bald (though geographically pinpointed) metaphysical speculation some of the poems toss off, as when he speaks of "the perception of forfeited paradise, which, once we have left it, / once we have lost it, looks like dirty old newsprint. I have / left in cloudy Umbrian mountains the knowledge that / what we once found is the vision that we lost / only because we found it." A poet beset by so many paradoxes as this might consider some of them well lost, as they seriously mar what is on the whole a book well worth reading. For, despite his grotesquerie and occasional absurdity—because of them, perhaps—he does say unprecedented things. It seems rather futile for critics to make reprimands, yet they consider doing so their prerogative. At age sixty-seven (and after so many books) Barker is surely aware that they are incorrigible; which need not prevent him from continuing to write as he pleases.

The "sweet reasonableness" of Robert Pinsky's *An Explanation of America** makes a sharp contrast with all of the above. We can doubt that the book does, in fact, explain America, but not that it defends the humane values of reason and communitarianism. It is not Pinsky's first such defense. Critic and poet, he is the author, first, of *Landor's Poetry* (1968), a book remarkable for the sensitivity, discrimination, and enthusiasm of its readings. It is also sometimes rash, as when Pinsky compares Landor's "To My Child Carlino" to Wordsworth's "Intimations" ode, with all the disadvantage on the side of Wordsworth. The same kind of rashness runs

*Princeton University Press, 1979.

through *The Situation of Poetry* (1975), Pinsky's survey of recent American poetry, with special reference to "Ode to a
Nightingale." The book argues interestingly but unconvinc-
ingly in favor of the "discursive" as a central poetic mode,
and the one most able to bear moral content. Within this polemical framework, Pinsky makes many aberrant judgments,
rating some poets too high, others—John Ashbery in particular—too low; and his treatment of Harold Bloom's views
exceeds, in tone and manner, what could be considered a legitimate expression of difference in critical opinion. In 1976
Pinsky published a book of poems, *Sadness and Happiness,*
which received high praise, and merited it. The title poem is
one of the best written in the 1970s; and the overall *convincing-
ness* of the book assures it of a readership for a long time to
come.

It is possibly Randall Jarrell who provided Pinsky with a
clue to the subject matter he has treated so tellingly in his
poetry, the aspirations and disappointments of Americans
"just like ourselves": dwellers in the suburbs, frequenters of
shopping malls, zoos, Pancake Houses; parents of fledgling
pianists and horsewomen, standers in line at the Savings and
Loan. There is a sweetness and pathos to all this—the
Cheever and Updike fictional turf—which has never been
captured so well before *in poetry.* The effect would be marred
if Pinsky had allowed himself to lapse into easy satire or sentimentality, or inaccuracy. His observations, like his style,
have an irrefutable air of honesty about them; so impressive
is the technical feat I'm tempted to apply to it something
Yvor Winters said (overstating a little) about Edwin
Arlington Robinson's poetry: "it is accurate with the consci-
entiousness of genius."

Accurate, truthful, conscientious: these are the terms that
describe Pinksy's poetry. Still, it must be said that *An Explanation of America* is a strange and irrational book in many of
its aspects. (I'm speaking of the long title poem, not the fine
short lyric "Lair," which opens the volume, nor the affecting
"Memorial," which closes it.) This long poem is strange

both in its ambitious scope and in the organization of its materials. It has three parts, titled "Its Many Fragments," "Its
Great Emptiness," and "Its Everlasting Possibility," each of
these in turn divided into four subtitled sections. The metric
frame throughout is rough iambic pentameter, with para-
graphing rather than fixed strophic breaks. The second part
of the poem includes a translation of Horace's *Epistula* I, xvi,
and a discussion of his life and thought. Pinsky's poem is
itself like an epistle, for he has subtitled it "A Poem to My
Daughter," (the "you" of the poem), and means it in some
sense to be addressed to her.

> I don't mean merely to *pretend* to write
> To you, yet don't mean either to pretend
> To say only what you might want to hear.
> I mean to write my idea of you,
> And not expecting you to read a word . . .

Every long poem needs a Beatrice, in this case the poet's
daughter. The fiction is useful here, allowing Pinsky to develop a colloquial or epistolary tone that *holds* the reader; I
have read the poem many times, and always straight
through, without stopping (this despite the obstacle of the
unvaried pentameter frame). The fact that the poet's inter-
locutor is a child and not an adult—his wife, for example,
whose entire absence from the poem is never explained—
helps support the general tone of simplicity, fairness, and
tact. Communing with ourselves, or addressing another
adult at length, we can't plausibly avoid defensiveness of one
sort or another—wisecracks, assertiveness, false modesty,
even ill humor. When children are listening, we have to do
better, and, given Pinsky's commitment to moral perspectives, he could hardly have found a better strategy.

The poem's narrator is present only as a voice and an observing eye, never as an actor; and this, too, helps keep intact
our confidence in his moral authority. Most people can see
and say what the right thing is, but few can plausibly present

themselves as doing it; or if they portray themselves as having erred, avoid the impression of self-hatred or self-pity.
None of the poet's actions, not even his profession, is given
in the text, and the inevitable complications are circum-
vented. Actually, the poet does, I believe, appear briefly in
the poem's third part, a scene where a father (presented in the
third person) watches his daughter's riding lesson. It is likely
that this character is really the poet, for the narrator (and
reader) are let inside his thoughts. It is the only such instance
in the poem, though, and even here the character is presented
primarily as an observer.

I raise these issues about the structure and intent of the
poem to emphasize the difficulty of the problems Pinsky has
had to contend with. He has risen to the challenge. Among
the many reasons to admire this book is its legitimate ambi-
tiousness; and I don't think it should be received as just one
more collection of poems, some good, some bad. "A country is the things it wants to see," we are told in the opening
part of the poem. Like Elizabeth Bishop, he has a keen eye;
and he can present what he sees, and, what's more, think
consequentially about it. At the mere level of perception, it
has already a vigorous, affecting clarity:

                                        . . . frowning,
    The children shuffled anxiously at command
    Through the home-stitched formations of the Square Dance.
    Chewing your nails, you couldn't get it straight.
    Another Leader, with her face exalted
    By something like a passion after order,
    Was roughly steering by the shoulders, each
    In turn, two victims: brilliant, incompetent you;
    And a tight, humiliated blonde, her daughter.

Thus he begins the characterization of his daughter, one of
the most winsome in any recent poem. Before it is ended,
you half wish she were your own daughter. "A country is
the things it wants to see," Pinsky says, and lists some of the

things she will become accustomed to, growing up as an American: all kinds of ball games, advertisements, Disney cartoons, *Deep Throat,* car crashes, Brownies (the Scouts, that is), collies, Colonial Diners, cute greeting cards, and "hippie restaurants." To be a snapper-up of unconsidered trifles on this scale is to have supreme confidence in the transforming power of lines in pentameter. Part of the fascination here is the nagging question of whether he has actually "gotten away with it." I think he has, partly because of the strange power of the "always-more-successful surrealism of everyday life," as Bishop once characterized it, and partly because of his use of incantatory, lulling repetitions of phrases and lines—a technique he may have borrowed from Bishop. As he moves through his topics, "Local Politics," "Countries and Explanations," his allusions as far-flung as Winston Churchill, Gogol, and Mayor Daley, one feels not so much instructed as chanted to, over a slowly, endlessly rocking cradle.

The most interesting part of the poem, conceptually and aesthetically, is the second, "Its Great Emptiness." The opening section, "A Love of Death," calls upon the reader to imagine a scene on the great Western plains (time unspecified), where a little girl is witnessing a communal grain harvest. As details are filled in, the imperative "imagine" is reiterated (some dozen times)—a device with precedents no less august than Canto XIII of the *Paradiso* and Bishop's "Little Exercise." These imaginings build up a powerful scene; the prairie takes on an hallucinatory solidity and presence, despite its having been carefully presented as fictive. Then, an untoward event: a half-crazed tramp climbs up on one of the threshing machines and throws himself into it; is killed. (I was reminded fleetingly of Kafka's "In the Penal Colony.") After this senseless occurrence, the scene dissolves, and the poem begins a meditation on the nature of the forces that might account for the atrocity, and others like it, on a philosophical or visionary level:

The obliterating strangeness and the spaces
Are as hard to imagine as the love of death . . .
Which is the love of an entire strangeness,
The contagious blankness of a quiet plain.
Imagine that a man, who had seen a prairie,
Should write a poem about a Dark or Shadow
That seemed to be both his, and the prairie's—as if
The shadow proved that he was not a man,
But something that lived in the quiet, like the grass.
Imagine that the man who writes that poem,
Stunned by the loneliness of that wide pelt,
Should prove to himself that he was like a shadow
Or like an animal living in the dark.

A possible antidote to these morbid imaginings of emptiness, dark, and death might, Pinsky proposes, be found in the consciousness of "immigrants and nomads":

And at the best such people,
However desperate, have a lightness of heart
That comes to the mind alert among its reasons,
A sense of the arbitrariness of the senses . . .
Like tribesmen living in a real place,
With their games, jokes or gossip, a love of skill
And commerce, they keep from loving the blank of death.

Another salutary outlook proposed is the traditional Horatian "equal mind"—and a sense of the *positive* value of death. Pinsky inserts into the poem Horace's Epistle to Quinctius, in which the genius of the Sabine Hills discusses their divergent modes of life and their chances for keeping dignity and uprightness. Horace observes that the man who is not afraid to die is safe from tyrants and an unworthy life—suicide is his warrant. The position may strike us as drastic, but it is true to the spirit of Stoicism and can name any number of precedents in Roman history. Pinsky's translation reads fluently and colloquially; he joins here the distinguished company of English translators of Horace, notably Sidney, Dryden, and Pope. *

The last part of "An Explanation of America" is its strangest. Here Pinsky takes up the issue of "everlasting possibility," that American theme, and juxtaposes it to a sense of limit and boundary. With only a tenuous sense of transition, he moves to an examination of evil, in its characteristic American form of violence. Random assault (with sexual connotations) and Vietnam are invoked. Pinsky views the Southeast Asia debacle as unprecedented, some sort of turning point in the national consciousness, a first loss of innocence. (But surely an earlier example is the 1860–1865 disaster, which still continues to deliver grievous consequences—reread *Patriotic Gore*.) If Pinsky fails to explain American violence, he can hardly be blamed; it is one of the country's ugly, unaccountable mysteries.

The poem comes to a close (three years after its author began it, we are told) with an engaging description of the young daughter performing the role of Mamilius in *The Winter's Tale,* suitably dignified in hose and tunic. This affectionate tableau of Romance is balanced, on the poet's side, by a fanciful panorama of an imagined mountaintop city; it is to be understood, I think, as a metaphoric portrait of America.

<blockquote>

On a lake
Beyond the fastness of a mountain pass
The Asian settlers built a dazzling city
Of terraced fountains and mosaic walls,
With rainbow-colored carp and garish birds
To adorn the public gardens. In the streets,
The artisans of feathers, bark or silk
Traded with trappers, with French and Spanish priests

</blockquote>

---

*For whatever reason the apologist of the *Aurea mediocritas* has never attracted many Americans, excepting writers like Franklin P. Adams, Louis Untermeyer, and Eugene Field—though I think I remember a version of the *Carpe diem* ode by Robinson, and a sonnet-length "imitation" in Lowell's *History*.

And Scottish grocers. From the distant peaks,
The fabulous creatures of the past descended
To barter or to take wives: minotaur
And centaur clattered on the cobbled streets
With Norseman and Gipsy; from the ocean floor
The mermaid courtesans came from Baltimore,
New Orleans, Galveston, their gilded aquaria
Tended by powdered Blacks. Nothing was lost—
Or rather, nothing seemed to begin or end
In ways they could remember. The Founders made
A Union mystic yet rational, and sudden,
As if suckled by the very wolf of Rome . . .

America having been summed up as "a pastoral / Delusion of
the dirt and rocks and trees, / Or daydream of Leviathan
himself, / A Romance of implausible rebirths," the poem
ends its long survey with a last glance at "our whole country,
/ So large, and strangely broken, and unforeseen."

My own survey of the poem doesn't do justice to its intri-
cacy and richness, the artful weaving of theme and metaphor
that makes for its dense, evocative texture. It is a poem in
which intellect and reason play a large role; the attendant
risks cannot be unfamiliar to the critic of Landor, whose
poem "To Barry Cornwall" reminds us:

> Reason is stout, but ever reason
> May walk too long in Rhyme's hot season:
> I have heard many folks aver
> They have caught horrid cold with her.

Still, to have more than usual intellect is a fate like any other;
if among the many mansions in the house of poetry there is
none to shelter that fate, then poetry is not as inclusive as we
believe—or need it to be. Myself, I consider "An Explanation of America" an important addition to American letters,
even if it goes against the grain in some ways.

I should mention as well one or two dislikes, since the
poem shows every sign of being able to weather them. The

title: wouldn't "Reflections on America" have been (though no more appetizing) more exact? Poets can sometimes explain the universe (which is ahistorical and nonspatial), but a country so large and various as ours is beyond their scope. The effort to contain and account for all our American experience is felt in this poem as effort; it could only be partially successful. Then, the contents: although the Epistle makes nice reading, bringing it and Horace's life into the poem strikes me as misjudged. The insights developed from them could have been presented in another fashion, one more consistent with the general plan and texture of the poem. And for obvious reasons, the biographical summary of Horace's life following the translation is filled with flat, prosy lines: "Time passed; the father died; the property / And business were lost, or confiscated." "Horace came back to Rome a pardoned rebel / In his late twenties, without cash or prospects. . . ." "I think that what the poet meant was this," (repeated later as, "I think that what the poet meant may be / Something like that"). These would be dull sentences even in a piece of prose.

No reader is likely to agree with all the opinions expressed or implied in the poem, of course. Pinsky is entitled to them; but I will mention one of his views that struck me as egregious. He describes an occasion when, during a flash flood on Chicago's Dan Ryan Expressway, "Black youths" appeared and "pillaged the stranded motorists like beached whales." He says, "a weight of lead / Sealed in their hearts was lighter for some minutes, / Amid the riot." This imaginative leap into the state of mind of the assailants may well be accurate; but why wasn't the same leap made in behalf of the victims in this case? The implied approval of the incident is unfortunate; this sort of spontaneism has never had the support of effective civil rights leaders, and is viewed by them as at most a futile reaction to present oppressive conditions.

Another surprising detail in the poem is Pinsky's misapprehension or simply abuse of some of Whitman's most ring-ing lines from "Crossing Brooklyn Ferry." After describing teenage prostitution in New York City, Pinsky continues:

> "It avails not,
> Time nor place, distance avails not"; the country shrugs,
> It is a cruel young profile from a coin,
> Innocent and immortal in the religion
> Of its own founding, and whatever happens
> In actual New York, it is not final,
> But a mere episode. . . .

This is a willful misuse of Whitman—a poet who, faced with a young prostitute and her "blackguard oaths," wrote, in *Song of Myself,* "Miserable! I do not laugh at your oaths nor jeer you."

The misuse is the more striking in that Pinsky himself owes quite a lot to Whitman—*An Explanation of America* is the most recent extension of that tradition, and one of the best. Pinsky is less sanguine than Whitman, of course; for more than a hundred years we have heard the melancholy, long, withdrawing roar of faith in the American Dream. But he shows, nevertheless, a reassuring agility of spirit and generosity of affections, inside and outside the domestic round. His discriminations and caveats deserve a careful hearing— the author of *Sadness and Happiness* and *An Explanation of America* is a very distinguished newcomer among the unruly tribe of our poets.

IV

HISTORY, GEOGRAPHY, VISION

History's Autobiography: Robert Lowell

Dante's praise is that he dared to write his autobiography in colossal cipher, or into universality.
            —Ralph Waldo Emerson, *"The Poet"*

—History, Steven said, is a nightmare from which I am trying to awake.
                        —James Joyce, *Ulysses*

Like most poets of stature, Robert Lowell takes his lead from several traditions. The early modernists just before him had done so. They absorbed continental Symbolism into a late nineteenth-century American tradition that had already (through Emerson, Poe, and Whitman) influenced French poets from Baudelaire to Mallarmé and Laforgue. This Franco-American hybrid was made to sort with late Victorian poetry, especially Browning; to answer as best it could to the rise of positivism and scientism; to look for values in Freud and Jung; and to strike back at the modern age with the help of Dada and Surrealist poetics. Surrealism is a late form of Symbolism, given a scientific base by Freud, a political theory by Marx, and a style of outrage by Dada. If Symbolism was a sort of *prélude* for the Word, scored for flute, harp, and fountain, Surrealist poetry was a café-concert vaudeville, accompanied by organ-grinder, biplane, and X ray.

THE American modernists used Surrealism each in a different way. Pound was the least affected by it, adopting just one of its techniques, radical juxtaposition; but he is much more

interested in *continuities* across time and space than the provocative Surrealist discontinuity. Stevens was drawn to some
of the Dadaist elements in Surrealism—its jarring humor, its
fantasy, its French—but he judged the unconscious to be
inadequate for poetry, and social revolution undesirable.
Williams liked the inclusiveness and unpredictability of
Surrealism—its Americanness, in short—but was more interested in daylight than in dreams. Eliot is probably the
most convinced Surrealist of these early innovators. The
Eliot of *The Waste Land* and *The Hollow Men* is, squarely,
a Surrealist, Dante and the English Renaissance notwith-
standing.

By the time Lowell began writing mature poems, most of
the Surrealists had lost interest in revolution. Moreover,
Eliot had declared himself to be classicist, Catholic, and roy-
alist, for once without apparent irony. His classicism meant,
in practice, a still more pronounced reliance on the English
tradition, and a giving over of Surrealism in favor of its root
form, Symbolism. *Ash Wednesday* and *The Four Quartets* are
Symbolist, not Surrealist poems. Several of the younger
modernists were to follow Eliot's lead, if not in politics, then
in religion and poetics. Auden's conversion to Christianity
was perhaps the most discussed, but there were others, in
some instances a simple renewal of faiths inactive since childhood. Robert Lowell, brought up as a lukewarm Episcopa-
lian, became a "firebreathing Catholic C.O.," confirmed
into the Roman church and marrying the Catholic Jean
Stafford almost at the same moment. Eventually and reluctantly, Allen Tate was to join the new faithful. One could say
that among the poets of the 1940s, Catholicism constituted
something of a freemasonry, a movable cell or sodality under
the benign supervision of Jacques Maritain. A spirit of the
catacombs made itself felt among these converts, who stood
in ardent, sometimes firebreathing opposition to the prevailing paganism around them, which they saw as responsible
for the disorder of contemporary society.

Lowell became a Roman Catholic modernist, inscribing

himself in a multiple tradition. His modernism emphasized the Catholic and Surrealist strains, in a way that can only have struck writers of conventional religious poetry as strange, not to say grotesque. Poems in *Land of Unlikeness* name the Virgin a "Hoyden" and Christ a "Drunkard," with no conscious will toward blasphemy. As for politics, Lowell liked to write about kings and to recall the kingship of Jesus, but he kept close to the left-liberal convictions that most American intellectuals had espoused in the thirties, without, to be sure, ever becoming a Stalinist. His politics were part of a program of historical consciousness. Eliot had urged such consciousness on all his disciples long before—though it is more literary than political history that preoccupied the author of "Tradition and the Individual Talent." Lowell adds to Eliot a consuming interest in nonliterary fact, from the present as well as the past. (Some of the same impulse can be noted in the "tape-recorded" bits of popular speech in *The Waste Land,* but much more prominently in the documentary texture of Williams's poetry.)

In Eliot's sensibility there were at work some of the forces of his Puritan heritage, its unremitting concern with the fallenness of human life, and a particular squeamishness concerning the body. In Lowell the Puritan legacy becomes even more pronounced. He could be expected to have negative feelings about the Bay Colonists from whom he and Eliot were descended, but to excoriate them as he did was dubious proof of being safely beyond their influence. Besides, the antihierarchical Congregationalist spirit could be felt as a valuable democratic tradition in American history, admirable even to those with no family connections to the New England Puritans. Also, some tenets of Calvinist theology prefigure and perhaps partly account for Lowell's devout interest in history. For the believer in predestination, every event on earth, small or great, is an expression of the divine will; it is capable of being deciphered if interrogated long enough. History is a factual allegory, not incompatible with newspapers and bookkeeping. Or so Cotton Mather argued in *Magnalia,* a detailed account of the flowering of Puritan religion in the New World, intended for the edification of Calvinist readers the world over. It showed how Providence had in one instance worked its design in human history, a pattern that was both earthly and divine. To be a practicing Puritan is to be a practical allegorist of human life.

Puritanism has its dark side: a constant dwelling on sin and damnation that sometimes resembles relish of them; an antipathy to Nature, especially to the body and appetitive pleasure. The Pauline and Calvinist quarrel with the material world was only intensified by specific conditions in the Bay Colony, where the natural environment, anything but pastoral, proved a deadly adversary. Something like a state of siege was the norm, lending extra vehemence to forces of repression in a small society that attempted, in any case, to approximate the absolutism of a theocracy. In this atmosphere of stricture and tension, outbreaks of irrationality could be counted on to appear, and so they did, both in the public and private realms. Witch hunts were perhaps the most horrible manifestation, but there were also chronic waves of revivalism and hysterical religiosity, in some ways comparable to the "born again" movements of our own day. The alert historical sense of Puritanism and its democratic premises were bound directly to a strain of repression, hysteria, and madness that contributed some violent chapters to American history.

Robert Lowell falls heir to the savage aspects of Puritanism as well as to its benign elements, though surely without intending to do so. It is not so much a matter of genes as simply having been reared in the old Bostonian milieu by parents who preserved good and bad traits from their ancestors and passed them on with no second thoughts. "91 Revere Street," Lowell's memoir about his childhood, has been read as a sort of prose *Prelude* that describes the making of a poet; it is also a case study in the origins of mental illness. For the misfortune of mania-depression, there was only one consolation. The "madness of art" was presumably connected to madness per se, and, if Surrealism had expanded the notion of what was intelligible, then Lowell's own psychic constitution might not be an insuperable disadvantage. Oneiric and violent imagery was never far from Lowell's consciousness, but Surrealist aesthetics taught him that this material could be used for art and in some sense be redeemed.

As a modernist, Lowell inherited not only the irrationality of Surrealism but also an enthusiasm for myth, which is also a vehicle of the irrational but one given structure by the logic of narrative. For Lowell, as for most artists, the single most important myth was the Orpheus story in all its variants. Its essential structure involves a descent into the underworld of death and then a restoration to life with added powers of understanding or skill. This framework underlies narratives as disparate as the Vergilian account of Aeneas's descent into Hades to consult the dead; Dante's *Inferno;* the Christian Passion, Descent into Hell, and Resurrection; and—in contemporary terms—any submersion in sleep, the unconscious, or even madness, with a subsequent reemergence into light, consciousness, and a renewal of imaginative power. Lowell made constant reference to classical myth during his first phase as a poet, and it remained a potent force in his writing throughout his career, sometimes openly and sometimes covertly. The most extended use of myth in his early phase came in *The Mills of the Kavanaughs,* constructed on the model of the story of Persephone, which is a female variant of the Orpheus myth. Later works follow the contour of the myth usually without directly naming it. The most characteristic moment in Lowell's poetry is going to sleep—or waking after a long sleep. Poems like "Falling Asleep over the Aeneid" and "The Lesson" show the author as he begins the Orphic descent; and more than a dozen other works depict him waking at sunrise to a painful lucidity that keeps, nonetheless, a low-level hangover of dream as part of the emotional tenor of the poem. (Among these poems, consider "Waking in the Blue," "Man and Wife," and "Ulysses and Circe.")

The several strains that went into the formation of Lowell's poetics and style—Symbolism, historical consciousness, Puritanism, Surrealism, Roman Catholicism, progressive politics, the documentary impulse—are by turns antithetical and reinforcing, and of course all of them had to be accommodated to the personal condition of mental illness. The story of Lowell's career is the record of changing emphases among these constitutive strains. Eventually the Roman Catholicism of early Lowell was abandoned—leaving behind some indelible marks—and the Williamsesque documentary impulse was given much greater prominence. There was, also, one final shift that had been only barely foreshadowed at the beginning—an involvement with American Romanticism as derived from Emerson.

Historical consciousness seems to be active in Lowell throughout his career, but even in his early phase it often took the form of documented autobiography. It is not easy for us now to revive the qualms and hesitations of poets in the early 1940s who wished to treat autobiographical subjects. They had to resolve for themselves Eliot's strictures in behalf of "impersonality." Was writing about oneself an exercise in vanity or futility? Perhaps it wasn't if one could show that personal experience was *representative* (which is not necessarily to say exemplary). Lowell felt he could write about himself if he stood for something more general than himself, at the level of myth or historical dialectic.

"Rebellion" is among the most explicitly autobiographical poems in early Lowell. Its subject—Lowell's knocking his father down—has an immediate scandalous interest, but Lowell was not satisfied with that. From the details of the poem we can see that it is his father's *house,* with its heirlooms and "chimney flintlock," as much as any person that is being brought down in the act of rebellion. Lowell labors to make this act represent a larger historical pattern: he stands for a principle of social change, militantly opposed to oppressive traditions associated with his family—mercantilism or capitalism, land-grabbing, and military violence. Well enough: but this covers only the first six pentameter lines of the poem. Several shorter lines follow, most of them in trimeter, then a pentameter couplet, some more short lines and a concluding pentameter. This second half of the poem describes a dream that follows the reported incident.

> Last night the moon was full:
> I dreamed the dead
> Caught at my knees and fell:
> And it was well
> With me, my father. Then
> Behemoth and Leviathan
> Devoured our mighty merchants. None could arm
> Or put to sea. O father, on my farm
> I added field to field
> And I have sealed
> An everlasting pact
> With Dives to contract
> The world that spreads in pain;
> But the world spread
> When the clubbed flintlock broke my father's brain.

Here is the Orphic descent into the irrational dream world, a recapitulation of what has already occurred in daylight. The shorter lines (notice the metrical "pun") outline Lowell's "pact" or "contract" to alleviate suffering in a world of pain. But the world of pain swells to full proportions again in the concluding pentameter, which recalls the poet's violence toward his own father and his tendentious use of the ancient heirloom weapon presented earlier as part of an ensemble symbolizing historical injustice. The poem's representative rebellion is seen as having been accomplished at the cost of violence, indeed, family violence—of adding to the universal sum of pain. This is the dilemma of the Christian revolutionary. Significant social change can come only at the cost of violence and suffering, in which the Christian can, in conscience, have no part. "Rebellion" also gives insight into some of the sources of Lowell's mental illness: the problem of actualized Oedipal aggression, guilt, and a need to return to an unconscious state in order to confront that guilt.

The idea that one's personal experience derives from larger patterns of history and economics is good Marxist doctrine and was shared by most intellectuals of the late thirties and early forties. That the unfolding of one's own life has a mythic and religious dimension is as old as human culture; but this belief had been discarded along with Christianity by the intellectuals of the second half of the nineteenth century. It returned in some of the secular but spiritual propositions of psychoanalysis and anthropology and was then brought under the Christian rubric with Eliot's and other modernists' conversion to Catholicism. Lowell gives the impression of having always remained at least theist, even after abandoning Roman Catholic faith in the early 1950s. (According to his wishes, his funeral offices were said at the Episcopal Church of the Advent in Boston.)

Whereas Eliot's reliance on Greek and Roman classical mythology was never large, not even as extensive as his debt to Dante, Lowell was from the first saturated with it. At Kenyon, he majored in classics and took his degree summa cum laude. His mentor Tate was a near example of Latinity in poetry, and of course the mixture of classical and Christian elements had impressive earlier precedents. It is the structural basis for the *Commedia,* and it is intrinsic to Milton's poetry as well as to much Neoclassical poetry in the seventeenth and eighteenth centuries. The same blending determined the structure and substance of *Ulysses,* which still somehow remained secular and was the modernists' favorite novel. *Ulysses* also incorporated personal and autobiographical matter and for that as well could serve as a model for the kind of poetry Lowell was to develop. Lowell's invocation of mythic or Christian perspectives always had, directly or indirectly, a bearing on the mere facts of his life. The notion that Eternity is in love with the works of Time can be applied in many ways. For Lowell, the Eternity of myth (pagan or Christian) has at last married Time (or history), and their child is Poetry (mythic autobiography)—"one life, one writing," as a later poem puts it. We can see why the early Lowell is entirely at home with Roman Catholicism, which, ideally, welds together the historical and mythic dimensions. Catholicism asserts on one hand that divine purpose is at work in historical evolution and on the other that there is an eternal dimension to experience that never changes, a dimension figured in the mass and in the succession of sacred seasons in the church calendar.

Life Studies marks the point in Lowell's poetry when classical and Christian references begin to retreat in favor of "mere" historical and autobiographical fact. "Beyond the Alps," the first poem in the volume, announces Lowell's renunciation of Roman Catholicism and in part tries to account for it. A parenthetical note after the title sets the poem "On the train from Rome to Paris. 1950, the year Pius XII defined the dogma of Mary's bodily assumption." We should not assume that it was solely the promulgation of a new dogma that led to Lowell's disaffection with the Roman church. For one thing, 1950 was the year of his father's death, as a poem placed later on in the volume mentions. This event, given the burden of guilt and confusion that Lowell's father represented, can only have come as a release to Lowell. The bolstering structures of Christian myth would then be needed commensurately less by the survivor.

At another level, the text of the poem makes it implicitly clear that for Lowell Roman Catholicism had become too provincial a system of belief to answer to the modern world and its record of violence and horror. So far from being the infallible spokesman on earth for Godhead, the pope is simply another mortal (who shaves each morning under the watchful gaze of his pet songbird). The papacy was unable or unwilling to halt the rise of Fascism; it must bear the guilt. And since, unlike individual popes or fathers, the papacy cannot die, Lowell sees his task as one of discreditation, by implied argument and overt satire. Moreover, when the poet turns his attention to the legacy of classical myth, it is found

to be of not much more use than religion. Lowell conflates
the cultural summit reached in ancient Greece with the Alps
or the then-unscalable Everest. "There were no tickets for
that altitude," not for moderns caught in the cultural disin-
tegrations of post–World War global society. Lowell goes a
step farther: he presents a negative version of Athena or
Minerva, goddess of wisdom and military skill. She is "pure
mind and murder at the scything prow— / Minerva, the miscarriage of the brain." This immaterial virgin, whose Par-
thenon is an unscalable mountain, offers no help to mid–
twentieth century citizens. Meanwhile it has been the fault of
the pope to take the very human, physical figure of Mary and
transform her into a purely mythic, otherworldly goddess.
This is a metaphoric way of summing up the failure of the
Church to keep its historical dimension alive and active.
Lowell sees it as retreating into pure myth and immateriality,
and hence irrelevant to him and the modern condition. But
his is no joyful deconversion. "Much against my will,"
Lowell says, "I left the City of God where it belongs."

The Church belongs "beyond the Alps," a local, cisalpine
Italian cult. The contemporary world, on the other hand,
was born in Paris, city of enlightenment, revolution, and art.
Between the second and third sonnets that make up this
poem, night comes on and the poem's speaker falls asleep.
When "Beyond the Alps" was first printed in *Partisan Review,* an extra sonnet stanza at this point described a dream of
the narrator. (Lowell reprinted the poem in *For the Union
Dead,* with the missing stanza restored.) The "dream" is a
quasi-Surrealist ramble in which the dreamer comes to speak
in the voice of the author of *Metamorphoses.* In *Life Studies'*s
shorter version, the dream sonnet is replaced by ellipsis, and
the poem goes directly to the poet's awakening—"kicking in
my berth," as he puts it. An overnight trip to Paris has been
metaphorically transformed into the Orphic descent and rebirth to waking reality, as the City of Light hoves into view:
"Paris, our black classic, breaking up / like killer kings on an
Etruscan cup." Lowell's ambivalent feelings toward the new

secular order are manifest here. If Paris is a "classic," it is also black. If it is like a cup (and not a chalice), still the image painted on it is of Etruscan "killer kings." The Etruscans were, of course, the first to use the emblem of the *fasces* adopted by Mussolini. In the official version of Roman history, the last Etruscan reign ended with Tarquinius Superbus, the father of the Tarquin of Shakespeare's *Rape of Lucrece*. In the legend, the elder Tarquin murdered his father-in-law so as to be proclaimed king. This deed, and the rape of Lucrece, so enraged the Roman people that Superbus in turn was assassinated, the monarchy scrapped, and the Roman Republic founded. To invoke him at the conclusion of the poem is to remind us of the burden of historical violence continuous from classical times to the present, which the Pax Romana sought to counteract. To give up hope in the personal and historical effectiveness of the Church is to be abandoned to history. The remainder of *Life Studies* is a working out of the implications, positive and negative, of this new, secular set of conditions.

The negative themes of *Life Studies*—apart from wars, murder, and tyrannical rulers—include the persistence of Victorian repressiveness, incarceration (of criminals or the insane), the "woe that is in marriage," death, the disorder of modern life, sexual maladjustments, and mental illness. By the mid-1950s, Lowell had come to recognize that manic episodes would almost certainly be chronic with him. If there could be no lasting cure for this ailment, perhaps some compensation for it could be found in applying his condition to the external world, seeing his illness as a truthful representation of that world. Madness might be felt as more than a private calamity, indeed, a symptom of universal madness in modern society. (I leave aside the question of whether seeing one's private condition as *representative* contains in itself a strain of madness.) As for Lowell's returns to health, did they betoken a recovery for society as well? Perhaps: if Lowell could survive a confrontation with misery and insanity, others might as well, in however small or great numbers. Lowell saw himself as going haltingly on, hand in hand with modern civilization, never certain when the next setback would come. His cures were temporary, chapters in a tale of patience and endurance. One sees that the temptation to suicide was great for him, yet he managed to outwit it, as though he had decided not to end his own life until the world's life came to an end, as was always possible after the development of nuclear armaments. Since Lowell equated his life as an artist with his life per se, work was a redemptive task for him; he kept to it constantly, turning his hand to translation and other literary tasks when subjects for poems were lacking. Part of the heroism to be found in Lowell's example is the heroism of work.

Apart from the labors of the artist, there are other forces that Lowell set into motion against the drift toward madness and suicide. From the evidence of the poetry alone, one can point to three qualities that Lowell associates with health: the drive toward prose; humor; and physicality, animal well-being. *Life Studies* marks an important thematic shift in Lowell's work, and it embodies as well a formal change for him, the use of a free-verse poetics. In poetry, he looked to the examples of Williams and Elizabeth Bishop but also adapted some of the virtues of prose writers like Flaubert and Chekhov—their careful observation and unheightened presentation—to his purposes. The volume includes a long prose memoir, "91 Revere Street," a title as factual as the texture of the memoir itself. Actually the very factuality of the piece is part of its humor; seldom has satire been based on circumstantial evidence so minutely detailed. The young Lowell comes in for ridicule as much as anyone else, but there is no hint of self-flagellation. Prose rhythms, conversational tone, humor, a constant recurrence of fact—these can all be used as counterforces to the hypnotic meter of poetry, its heightened diction and presentment, its swelling emotions, the undertow toward fantasy and dream. When poetry seemed like a mild or not so mild form of hallucination, the chronically ill poet might look to the prosaic elements in verbal art as a steadying antidote, turning to the prescriptions of, say, Chekhov so as to bolster the reality principle. Beyond that, the cultural spokesman in Lowell allows *Life Studies* to register the extent to which he felt that the peculiar qualities of poetry had been supplanted by prose strategies in contemporary writing. A decline in the prestige of religious myth will necessarily bring along with it a decline in the prestige of metrical form: among the things Lowell finds beyond the Alps is free verse. Even though it is poetry he continues to write, not prose fiction or nonfiction, the relationship of his poetry to prose is always strong after *Life Studies*. And we recall, incidentally, that all three women to whom Lowell was married were prose writers.

The careful plotting of *Life Studies,* with its many significant leitmotifs and balanced pairings, its color themes and its echoes, can persuade us that a poetry based on prose need not lose richness and complexity. The book is awash in factual detail, but the wonder is just how much Lowell makes his details cooperate and signify. Objects apparently modest and empty of signification are often found, on closer inspection, to have subterranean connections with a larger system of meaning. The ingenuity with which Lowell draws out these themes may remind us of paranoid fantasy, and if so perhaps we can see it as one more example of Lowell's turning a personal flaw into a poetic strength. Has anyone looked closely, for instance, at *Life Studies*'s garbage cans? In "91 Revere Street" we are told that the narrator's father painted the label "R. T. S. Lowell—U.S.N." on his family's personal receptacles. No explicit comment is made in the memoir; perhaps it is an amusingly pathetic detail put in for the humor. But, when the poet (in "Memories of West Street and Lepke") mentions seeing a man scavenging the garbage can behind his house on "hardly passionate Marlborough Street," we begin to wonder. Finally, when Lowell concludes "Skunk Hour" with the image of a mother skunk plundering a garbage pail to find sustenance for herself and her kittens, we know the poet is up to something.

Eliot's *Waste Land* was a landscape of "stony rubbish," a "heap of broken images," or an "Unreal City," where crowds of humanity are felt to be simply one more disposable waste product—but where, also, fragments can be shored against the ruin of self and society. The junk pile interested Stevens, too, who viewed modern consciousness as a "Man on the Dump," thought rooting among discarded images and "mattresses of the dead" to find some wherewithal for continuing life. Lowell's response to the scrapheap of history is to follow the skunk's lead, to dig into the garbage of experience, personal and historical, no matter how miscellaneous or ugly, and to wring sustenance from it. The Etruscan cup of "Beyond the Alps" (as J. D. McClatchy has pointed out) is replaced by a cup of sour cream in the last poem of *Life Studies*. The mother skunk jabs her head into it, feeds, and "will not scare." The skunk's fearlessness, her rich animality, are presented as saving qualities in a world of disorder and madness. And she is female. The refreshing and commonsense qualities of women rank very high for Lowell. The ability to appreciate physical life he associated with Elizabeth Bishop, to whom the poem is dedicated. In any case, the warm, mammalian version of womanhood is seen as a positive counterpart to cold goddess figures, statuary or immaterial, like Minerva, "pure mind and murder," "the miscarriage of the brain."

After *Life Studies*, Lowell published *Imitations*, a collection of translations from many languages and periods. Lowell seems to have anticipated the criticism it would receive for the "inaccuracy" of his renderings—he does not call the book *Selected Translations*. In effect he has made new Lowell poems at the instigation of the originals, an approach as old as the English Renaissance. "Imitation," as opposed to strict translation, is of course a way of making the fixity and otherness of non-English poetry from the past susceptible to time and change, of, so to speak, taking an art work out of the Louvre and bringing it into one's own house. In Lowell's case, this kind of translation amounts to colonizing other literary traditions with personal contemporaneity, appropriating them to an expanded notion of the self. *Imitations* contains in germ the scope and intention behind Lowell's "epic," *History,* which took the most of Western culture, its political as well as its literary record, as Lowell's province.

Several more steps, though, were needed before Lowell arrived at the threshold of this grand project. The title poem of *For the Union Dead* inaugurates that more active role Lowell was to take in American politics of the 1960s. As a citizen and as a poet, Lowell was to strike blows, first, in favor of the civil rights movement and then against United States involvement in the Vietnam war. The record of private and public life found in *Near the Ocean* and *Notebook 1967–1968* by turns stuns and leaves us indifferent, as Lowell succeeds well or poorly in the task of joining the two realms into a convincing poetry. Political activism brought Lowell a fame or notoriety outside the purely literary realm. People who had never read so much as a word of his poetry came to recognize the participant in the 1967 march on the Pentagon and the campaign supporter of Eugene McCarthy. The distractions that went with political activism seem to have been outweighed, in Lowell's case, by the pleasure of making history—and from history, literature. Lowell said it was the Pentagon march that inspired him to take up writing *Notebook 1967–1968*. The expanded and revised *Notebook* came out in 1970, to be followed by yet a third redaction, which was larger still and moreover had calved with two attendant volumes *(For Lizzie and Harriet* and *The Dolphin)* made up of poems pruned from the earlier *Notebook.* This startling literary event (the books all appeared in 1973) brings us to the final phase, or next-to-final phase, in Lowell's career. *History* embodies Lowell's sense of what he had accomplished from the beginning of his career up to that time.

History and the *Notebooks* that led up to it mark another stylistic shift in Lowell, a new adaptation of Surrealism to his purposes. American poetry at large in the sixties had turned toward Surrealism, of a Latin American rather than a French variety, and the sensitive barometer of Lowell's attention to actuality had registered this change. In his "Afterthought" to the first *Notebook,* he said, "I lean heavily to the rational, but am devoted to surrealism." The difference between heavy leaning and devotion is like the contrast between the reality principle and aspiration. The *Notebooks* are suffused with an irrationality of a peculiar Lowellian variety, the origins of it going all the way back to his early work. In the revised *Notebook,* he was to change his "Afterthought" in several particulars, substituting the word "unrealism" for "surrealism." He thereby recognizes the differences between his own mode and that of the other American surrealists. This telling difference, moreover, is epitomized in a word from the vocabulary of Wallace Stevens, philosopher-poet of the realized "unreal." By the late 1960s, Lowell had become interested again in the American Romantic tradition, the one that runs from Emerson through Whitman, Dickinson, Crane, and Stevens. Of course the interest in Crane and Emerson had been present from the beginning of Lowell's career. There is a poem to Emerson in *Land of Unlikeness,* and he is the leading light of "Concord" in Lowell's next book. Lowell had inherited Crane through inclination and the example of Allen Tate. Although the poem to Crane in *Life Studies* gives an aberrant portrait of Crane, it still testifies to a deep fascination with him. Whitman, Lowell more than once singled out as America's "best poet." And Lowell had admired Stevens as early as the publication of *Transport to Summer,* which he reviewed for *The Nation* in 1947, calling Stevens "one of the best poets of the past half-century." Emerson and Whitman had been generally in discredit with Lowell's mentors (Tate and Ransom) when he began writing. The Eliotic-aristocratic-Agrarian poets saw Emerson as having contributed to the paganism, optimism, and market mentality that had all but wrecked the American experiment, and they considered Whitman's ideals of democracy indiscriminate and unrealistic. But so multiple, so Protean a figure as Lowell could still draw on a potential relationship to the central American Romantics, and this tradition was activated within him as strongly as it could ever be in *History*.

Lowell's book is a startling literary realization of Emerson's views on the proper stance that his ideally self-reliant representative man should take toward history. Consider these statements from the essay "History": "There is one mind common to all men. Every man is an inlet to the same and to all of the same." "Man is explicable by nothing less than all his history." "Each new fact in [individual man's] private experience flashes a light on what great bodies of men have done, and the crises of his life refer to national crises." "The student is to read history actively and not passively; to esteem his own life the text, and books the commentary." "All history becomes subjective; in other words, there is properly no history, only biography."

History might just as well been called *The Lowelliad,* though of course that would have put off readers. Lowell was content to suggest that for all its range of reference, it is still "his story"—and hence so much more than that. One can substitute the author's name for the word "History," which opens the first line of the sequence's opening poem: "[Lowell] has to live with what was here," and go on to substitute "I" for "we": "Clutching and close to fumbling all [I] had— / it is so dull and gruesome how [I] die, / unlike writing, life never finishes." In fact, by the end of the poem, pronouns are changed to singular in the text: "my eyes, my mouth, between them a skull's no-nose— / O there's a terrifying innocence in my face. . . ."

These opening pages labor, as David Kalstone has observed, to make the characteristically Lowellian moment of awakening fuse with the dawn of human consciousness. The fourth poem of the sequence, titled "Dawn," brings in "Adam and Eve, adventuring from the ache / of the first sleep" to enhance Lowell's perception of how he feels waking next to his wife, "early Sunday morning in New York— / the sun on high burning, and most care dead." The sequence passes through several Biblical subjects (Cain and Abel, King David), intermingling them with personal observations and appropriations. The sixteenth sonnet (a translation of Valéry's "Hélène," first published in *Imitations*) introduces the Hellenic tradition, rich with monuments Lowell claims as his own. Still, we cannot avoid a moment of shock when we see a statement belonging to Lowell's mother (as recorded in "91 Revere Street") ascribed, in the twenty-first sonnet, to Clytemnestra. "I usually / manage to make myself pretty comfortable," is the conclusion to a long speech not found in the earlier prose work but, even so, entirely consonant with what we know about Mrs. Lowell. "Clytemnestra 1" is followed by sonnets "Clytemnestra 2" and "Clytemnestra 3," these two hewing much closer to the original mythic subject. We can, however, no longer read them "innocently"; each detail is sifted and weighed for autobiographical and psychological meaning.

A "stereoscopic" reading of *History* yields the most coherent understanding of Lowell's autobiographical epic, so long as the component strands remain in balance. Curious overlaps appear. Of the two sections devoted to Caligula, the first is a distant version of Baudelaire's "Spleen," translated line for line by Lowell a decade earlier but now cut down to sonnet size and attributed to the mad Roman emperor. The second Caligula section is also a reduced and reworded version of an earlier poem (from *For the Union Dead),* in which Lowell reflects on the monstrous historical figure childhood schoolmates had likened him to—indeed, going so far as to nickname him "Cal." (This was the name he was familiarly called by the rest of his life.)

History first makes an overwhelming impression of inclusiveness, but, after that has subsided, we can observe just how little of its field it draws upon. Aside from the Far East's being utterly disregarded, we note that Western history up to the twentieth century takes up only the first half of the book. The remainder corresponds roughly with Lowell's own life-span from 1917 to the late 1960s. Taking a census of the first half shows that more subjects are drawn from French history and culture than from English or American. Napoleon receives more attention than Washington and Jefferson combined. Literature counts as much as political history; a sonnet of Baudelaire weighs as heavily in the sum total as the entire career of Mohammed. Also, despite the abundant erudition, mistakes now and then creep in—as when Lowell conflates the seventeenth-century French poet Malherbe with the eighteenth-century *encyclopédiste* Malesherbes ("Malesherbes, l'Homme de Lettres"). Closing the book, anyone not hushed by erudition into uncritical reverence will surely feel much more the idiosyncrasy of the sequence than its universality. But of course Lowell intended a personal, Emersonian "epic," not a general one.

To treat the *Notebooks* and their culmination in *History* as Lowell's *Leaves of Grass* asks us not only to see the development of a personal epic, but also to follow on the track of another intention. Just as any writer has a personal history— his autobiography—a body of work has its history, too—the developing contour of a career. The *Notebook-History* trio stands, among other things, for Lowell's changing sense of what he had achieved in poetry, under the influence of three temporal forces: modern political events; his own life story (marriages, displacements, work, fatherhood, aging, fame); and, finally, the deployment and evolution of his own talents as a poet as they unfolded in the shifting climate of American literature. Even the first *Notebook* revisits themes from earlier Lowell. The second *Notebook* revisits these revisitings; and *History* returns again to this twice-spaded soil. In all three cases, the reworkings amount to a continuous reevaluation by Lowell of the shape and meaning of his own career. He seems to have been trying to embody in his work a metaphysical fable about Time and Writing. Time has made him one more reader of his poetry and so, inevitably, into a reviser of it.

The actual specific terms of this rewriting will some day be worked out in close detail. Most critics have declined the challenge of *History*. The "unrealism" or hallucinatory impressionism of Lowell's compositional habits in the sequence do of course put obstacles in the path of understanding. Yet that very inwardness, knotty and recalcitrant, is inseparable from the power of *History;* and an important question is whether eventual decipherment will render the sequence less arresting and provocative or add range and meaning to it.

History did not put the final seal on Lowell's achievement. In 1976 a *Selected Poems* appeared, with poems taken from all his books up to and including *History* and the companion volumes published in 1973. This selection (which involved a few revisions) amounts to yet another assessment by Lowell of the shape and meaning of his career—which comes to seem like the literary equivalent of a "mobile," with constantly shifting relationships between its parts. Lowell saw life as "pure flux," and he wanted poetry to come as close to life as is consistent with artistic order. The extremely elaborate relationship of his writings *to themselves* adds a new quality of unfixity to a work already complex and diverse. Lowell's last book, *Day by Day* (1977), was much simpler in style than its recent forerunners; and in it autobiography and classical myth again came forward as chief structural elements. Was Lowell entering a new stylistic phase? The book may have been the first step in a return from the Emersonian "Orphism" of *History*. As matters stand, *Day by Day* comes only as a coda to the rest of Lowell's work, not really changing our sense of what he had accomplished. Or at least not yet: unlike life, writing and reading never finish.

Robert Lowell died in 1977. He is buried in Dunbarton, New Hampshire, among the gray headstones of his Stark, Winslow, and Lowell relatives, a "suave Venetian Christ" in quiet surveillance over all. Lowell's own monument, in pink marble, bears the inscription, "The immortal is scraped unconsenting from the mortal." A characteristic reversal of graveyard sentiment, this is a good summary of Lowell's work as well as his life. His whole effort as a poet was bent toward welding these irreconcilables into one poetry—eternizing the transitory *and* making sure that gray eternity was kept in the pink of health and life.

12

Elizabeth Bishop's Nativities

"More delicate than the historians' are the map-makers' colors," says the concluding line of "The Map," on the opening page of Elizabeth Bishop's *Collected Poems*. "Delicate" here keeps its double meaning of "pleasing" and "vulnerable." Much of this poet's effort can be summed up as putting delight ahead of instruction in the scale of values—or, paradoxically, asking us to recognize that delight is one of the most important things we can learn, one of the few antidotes to pain and the experience of dread. To keep delight at its freshest, she would rid poetry of as much armoring as possible. "The Armadillo," a poem dedicated to Robert Lowell, takes up this theme in an almost Aesopian manner: the armadillo's habits have human counterparts. She describes the embattled mammal as *"a weak mailed fist / clenched ignorant against the sky."* If armor protects weakness and ignorance, those who wear it tell us more about themselves than they know. Armor and coats of mail appear several times in Bishop's poetry, and it isn't solely the sonic coincidence of "mail" with "male" that leads her to associate men and warfare. Bishop sees the masculine readiness for combat in many contexts, however, not in military engagements alone; these are only its most extreme, its most physically destructive instances. Actually, any sort of browbeating, lecturing, or oratory she perceives as an illegitimate use of force, whether in life or poetry.

Bishop has been quoted (in a letter to Anne Stevenson, published in the March 7, 1980, *Times Literary Supplement*) on this subject: "I don't much care for the grand, all out efforts (in art) but on the other hand I sometimes *do*. . . . I admire Robert Lowell's poetry very much and much of *Lord Weary's Castle* couldn't be more all out. . . . He and I have been friends since 1946." Although Bishop and Lowell were friends, he represented something that she wanted to define herself against, and the difference is partly signaled in the title of her last book. *Geography III,* which makes us think of a child's textbook, was Bishop's response to Lowell's ambitious sequence *History,* published four years earlier.

Bishop did, however, write one "all out" poem herself, where the combative instincts of an emblematic fowl are made to have as wide relevance as possible. In "Roosters," when she begins piecing together her description, mentioning "cruel feet," "stupid eyes," "uncontrolled, traditional cries"; when she asks, "what right have you to give / commands and tell us how to live . . . and wake us here where are / unwanted love, conceit and war?" and styles the cockscomb as a "virile presence," "charged with all your fighting blood"; when she has said as much and more, the roosters may conclude that they are not the only combative creatures round about. Bishop seems to be aware of the internal contradiction. In the second part of the poem she begins to try to resolve it, first by reminding us that in Christian iconography the cock has come to symbolize forgiveness, by association with the story of Saint Peter's triple denial of Christ (and eventual repentance). "There is inescapable hope," she says, and one can only hope she is right.

She goes further still. In the coda of the poem (the last fifteen lines), she asks, "how could the night have come to grief?" and begins to hint that the "we" of the poem might have participated in a form of violence comparable to the roosters'. Someone has been harmed, as the final tercet implies: "The sun climbs in, / following 'to see the end,' / faithful as enemy, or friend." Bishop is quoting from Matthew 26:58, where Peter joins a crowd assembled at the high priest's palace after Jesus's arrest, "to see the end." How to interpret this second reference to Peter's betrayal? And in what sense can an enemy be faithful? The notion of a faithful enemy bears the same kind of ironic tension as the phrase "inescapable hope." Keeping in mind Blake's dictum that "opposition is true friendship," and allowing for the possibility that "sun" is a pun for the Son of God, or simply stands as an emblem of purification, we can see a reversal of roles here. Jesus is also interested to know how the "story" ends; he is as much concerned with Peter's conduct in the courtyard of the palace as with the proceedings inside. An enemy to Peter's failings, still to Peter himself he is a friend. It is this attitude that Bishop wants to appropriate in the poem, a judgment outweighed by mercy—and not merely with respect to others but also to herself. If the poem has been at pains to discover in the cock not only an emblem of violence but also a symbol of hope, part of this effort is to teach the author that her own conflicts, as they belong to a universal pattern of violence, may also share in the "inescapable hope" and find a resolution.

When "Roosters" was printed in Bishop's first book, she appended the date "1941" to it, no doubt to remind us it was written during a world war and to emphasize that private, human violence is only a small instance of a problem international in scope. Acceding to the one amounts to fostering the other; therefore one should first look to the private realm before making public statements. More important for a poet, the private realm is where violence is undergone in its least abstract form. Another letter to Anne Stevenson says, "My outlook is pessimistic. I think we are still barbarians who commit a hundred indecencies and cruelties every day of our lives, as just possibly future ages may be able to see. But I think we should be gay in spite of it, sometimes even giddy—to make life endurable and to keep ourselves 'new, tender, quick.'" (Bishop is quoting from the last line of Her-

bert's "Love Unknown.") *"We* are barbarians," she says, im-
plying that she numbers herself among those who should be
better, just as she does in "Roosters." The problem of recon-
ciling this unsparing self-knowledge with a strong wish to
write a poetry with moral dimensions became the substance
of many poems after "Roosters." More and more Bishop
moves toward a mode of *self*-teaching—but of course this
delicate form of instruction is available to any reader who
cares to make use of it. The gaiety she recommends is the
Nietzchean, tragicomic spirit that Yeats describes in "Lapis
Lazuli." His models "Do not break up their lines to weep. /
They know that Hamlet and Lear are gay; / Gaiety trans-
figuring all that dread." And dread can be transfigured into,
among other things, poetry.

Milder than "Roosters" and yet still a sharp criticism of
spiritual violence is the poem "Seascape." Bishop's method
here is to work out a careful ecstasy within the "celestial seascape" of the poem, pressing lightly on the natural beauty of
the scene. Particular details take on a paradisal aura: the her-
ons are "angels" with "immaculate reflections"; there are
"Gothic arches" among the mangrove roots, "illumination"
on the leaves. It is all like a "tapestry for a Pope"; "it does
look like heaven." Even so, one feature jars: the lighthouse,
painted black and white. Bishop personifies this man-made
intruder as a preacher in clerical dress, a preacher unaware of
the "celestial" beauty around him. He is preoccupied more
with hell than with heaven; and even heaven, in his version,
"has something to do with blackness and a strong glare."
When night falls, he will "remember" (not discover or invent) "something strongly worded to say on the subject."
Bishop makes us share her dislike for the baleful emblem; and
yet her own intolerance here is not altogether different from
the lighthouse-preacher's. Perhaps we can now see more
clearly just how Bishop is caught in the moralist's dilemma.
How can a poem attack violence, or how condemn the habit
of condemning, without compromising itself? Bishop must

have been conscious that she carried a variant of "Seascape"'s castigating preacher with her on all her travels; and a good part of the effort in her poems is to exorcise him, using whatever means—apart from the "barbaric"—available to her. She must not only learn to teach herself rather than others; she must make certain that this teacher in no way resembles the martinet or the hanging judge.

The first half of "Seascape" is an early solution to the problem of right teaching. By a careful enumeration of visual particulars and by the invention of a series of related metaphors (imaging the idea of "heaven"), she assigns value to sense perception: it is a positive good, and so is the ability to find striking metaphoric equivalences for what she sees. Bishop comes back to this lesson over and again in her poetry. If she needed precedents for her aesthetic of visual appreciation, no doubt she could have cited Thomson: "A minute and particular enumeration of circumstances judiciously selected, is what chiefly discriminates poetry from history and renders the former, for that reason, a more faithful representation of nature than the latter"; or Blake: "Singular and Particular Detail is the foundation of the Sublime." And then nineteenth-century poetry would have offered her a gallery of visual poems under many rubrics, from the Pre-Raphaelitism of Rossetti's "The Woodspurge," to Browning's frankly celebratory "The Englishman in Italy," to Hopkins's "Pied Beauty." Bishop's debt to Imagism and to Marianne Moore's poems of visual detail has often been discussed, and it is real. Yet neither Moore nor Bishop is finally an Imagist. Both poets considered visual perception and accurate description values in themselves, but both were also concerned to bring other values into poetry as well. "The power of the visible is the invisible," Moore said. This makes the relative value of visible and invisible realms into something of a tangle—so much so that Bishop found sorting it out a lifetime's occupation. The result is a long series of lessons delicately self-taught, lessons of serious importance to follow.

The mixture of visual particularity and other concerns not visible begins in "The Map," a useful early key for reading Bishop. The title is not "The Map of Nova Scotia" or "The Map of the U.S.A.," so we see at the outset that allegorizing energies are at work. The poem has three stanzas, the first and last composed in eight rhymed lines, some of the rhymes identical words. This "trope of rhyme" here stands for the process of mapping itself, whereby differently colored areas on a printed page are meant to "rhyme" with the vastly larger shapes of continents and oceans. The poem's middle stanza, however, is several lines longer than the others and has no rhyme. It brings in the observer, under the characteristic Bishop first-person plural, who appears, overtly, nowhere else in the poem. "We can stroke these lovely bays," she says, evoking an active engagement with the map under inspection. The poem never states just how much of the globe is being considered; Newfoundland, Labrador, and Norway, the only proper names mentioned, belong, however, to the Northern Hemisphere, indeed, to its most northerly part. The first stanza mentions no proper names, nor does it seem to deal with maps at all, but rather with the relationship between land and water. Only because of the title would a reader think these lines had anything to do with cartography. The realia mentioned (for example, "seaweeded ledges") are not actually visible in maps. Implied personification in the lines, "Or does the land lean down to lift the sea from under, / drawing it unperturbed around itself?" confirms the allegorical stance suggested in the title. Yet, even at the fabulistic level, one would think, Bishop has it backward. Shouldn't the water be "tugging at the land from under"? Not in this allegory, for land and water begin to signify here the conscious and unconscious mind. In Genesis, God divides the sea from the dry land, a deed that stands at the beginning of a long series of similar sacred reenactments—the sparing of Noah, or the Israelites' crossing the Red Sea, for example. But for the practicing poet, this primal division must be in part reversed; the conscious mind must reach down into the unconscious and bring up what is there. Bishop presents the land as more *volitional* than water; and after all, the Genesis association of dry land with conscious humanity does not strike even modern readers as arbitrary.

In stanza two appears the first specific place name, New-foundland (i.e., *new found land),* as though it had just emerged from the sea. A human being appears, "the moony Eskimo," a more welcome inhabitant than, say, the cler-gyman-lighthouse in "Seascape." Human engagement with topography first takes the fanciful form of presenting a La-brador "oiled" and made yellow by the Eskimo. In the same vein, stroking "these lovely bays, / under a glass" (a magni-fying glass) might be expected to yield results as surprising. How to interpret lines two through five of the second stanza? Perhaps "bays" is a pun for laurel leaves—think of Herbert's "Is the year only lost to me? / Have I no bays to crown it?" ("The Collar"). That would explain the "blossom" of the next line and would constitute an old-fashioned emblem for poetic triumph. The magnifying glass could stand for the kind of inspection that must be brought to bear on a subject in order to see its potential for meaning. In what sense, then, could it also "provide a clean cage for invisible fish"? Perhaps in the sense that not all the meanings of a subject can be ren-dered visually or made easily accessible. Pondering the im-plications of "clean cage," the reader may decide to allow these fish to remain invisible, and some of the poem's possi-ble range of meanings be left implicit.

Further inventions and clues: the names of seashore towns run out to the less settled realm of the sea, "the printer here experiencing the same excitement / as when emotion too far exceeds its cause." That, of course, is the classic definition of sentimentality. Any poet schooled in the 1930s, the era of modernist criticism, would be very much on her guard against it. And yet Bishop does not really disparage the printer. She feels some of his excitement herself—just as she seems to share the anxiousness of the hare in stanza three (the map of Norway) that "runs to the south in agitation." To complete stanza two, we are given one more metaphor for the interaction of land and water—the peninsulas that "take the water between thumb and finger / like women feeling for the smoothness of yard-goods"—and that homely personification allows for a transition, by way of water's silken smoothness, to the poem's conclusion.

"Mapped waters are more quiet than the land is, / lending the land their waves' own conformation." Here the allegory shows us that mapping (poetry) makes the sea (the unconscious) smoother than the land (the conscious mind). Wave motion is ironed out of the sea and appears on the land, in the form of the shading used to render mountain ranges. This wavy "conformation" is also a confirmation, for the two realms validate each other. "Mapping" calms one part of the mind and stirs up another, no doubt with desirable results. The immediate outcome in the poem is to set "Norway's hare" on his southward journey, and to insure that "profiles investigate the sea, where land is." (We remember that this first book's title, *North & South*, prefigures a sequence of poems following a path from Canada to New York and then to Florida.)

Suddenly the poem takes up a new subject: the poet wonders, perhaps because the hare has led her to scan several latitudes, what governs the map-makers' choice of colors for different countries: "are they assigned"? She clearly would prefer that the countries choose their own colors, according to "What suits the character or the native waters best." Poets write in accordance with what is "native" to themselves and to the landscape in which the poem is composed, choosing "colors" felt as appropriate to the subject. Also, "Topography displays no favorites." The paronomasia of "displays" (instead of "plays") allows both meanings to work: map-making neither bets on sure things nor features one country over another. Yet when the poem says, "North's as near as

West," it stakes a claim for the author of *North & South*. World history is the record of the westward movement of civilization; but this is not Bishop's subject. "More delicate than the historians' are the map-makers' colors." She will write "geography," not "history."

Keeping in mind that the sea, for Bishop, is an emblem for the unconscious helps decipher many poems coming after "The Map." Even a poem so late as "Questions of Travel," set in the interior of Brazil, brings in imagery of the sea, and for some of the same purposes as in the earlier poem. But sea imagery will have other resonances as well, and to consider them, I turn to "At the Fishhouses" in Bishop's second collection. At first glance a "realistic" poem, in fact it develops an allegory perhaps even more thoroughgoing than "The Map." After her first book, Bishop almost entirely abandons the dreamlike fable as a poetic mode in favor of concrete scenes and short narratives that have subtexts or allegorical overtones. Bishop seems to have devoted as much effort to rendering her realistic surfaces as to developing an underlying fable. The poems in this mode offer many pleasures at the level of apt sensory and metaphoric presentation alone, which for Bishop always keeps a positive value. The opening twenty-five lines of "At the Fishhouses" have been cited as among the most beautiful descriptions in modern poetry; but part of their power resides in the plausibility *and* surprising resonance of the details recorded.

For one thing, Bishop takes care to note as many jarring as beautiful aspects of the scene. The air smells of codfish; the rocks are "jagged"; the fish tubs are lined with "creamy iridescent coats of mail," but with "small iridescent flies crawling on them." This long, slow opening section is presented "objectively," the narrator discernible only in the impersonal pronoun "one." Otherwise, the scene includes no human agents, except for the old fisherman, hard at work repairing his net, however cold the day or late the hour. Much of the observed detail goes to emphasize the harshness of his life. At his age he is still working, and we see what some of his tasks must be—in, for example, the evidence offered by his "worn and polished" shuttle and the "narrow cleated gangplanks" along which wheelbarrows have to be pushed, up to "storerooms in the gables." There is also the silver presence of the sea, "swelling slowly as if considering spilling over." Of course a fisherman lives under constant threat of death, as we are reminded when the narrator mentions the "ancient wooden capstan" with its "melancholy stains, like dried blood."

The narrator herself begins to act and speak (and use the first-person pronoun) only toward the end of the opening section. She says, "The old man accepts a Lucky Strike. / He was a friend of my grandfather." He neither takes nor refuses: he *accepts*, a verb that tempers some of the irony present in the cigarette brand name. Bishop seems to feel a kinship with this fisherman, if only for the reason that "He was a friend of my grandfather." The past tense here lets us know that her grandfather is dead; therefore his coeval, the fisherman, is old enough to expect death at any time. "We talk of the decline in the population," says the next line, a somber topic in this context, with a hint of black humor. The surface sense of the statement (that the population of rural areas declined during the first part of this century because of young people's flight to cities—including Elizabeth Bishop's) registers with an extra edge. Even at his age the fisherman "waits for a herring boat to come in." But his ship will never come in; he will never have a "lucky strike"; and the ship approaching is, figuratively, the Ship of Death. The narrator focuses on his "black old knife, / the blade of which is almost worn away." The regular pentameter of this last line underlines the rhythmic repetitiveness of his daily task of scraping fish scales. Also, we are made to sense that the old man has roughly as long to live as his blade lasts, a blade almost worn away.

At this point the first paragraph change in the poem appears. The fisherman is never mentioned again—which, along with the break in the text, makes palpable his imminent death. And what does Bishop's narrator look at next? The water's edge, with tree trunks leading down under it. They are "laid horizontally / across the gray stones, down and down / at intervals of four or five feet." Or six feet, for that matter, the canonical depth of burial. In any case, we can hear funereal resonances in "laid horizontally," "gray stones," and "down and down" as well. The traditional expression here would be "Davy Jones' locker."

The next verse paragraph begins with a description of nearby water, which, if it is associated with the unconscious, must also now be assimilated to the idea of death. "Cold dark deep and absolutely clear, / element bearable to no mortal": Bishop characterizes the sea with a string of adjectives not set off by commas, as though presenting a new substance *colddarkdeep*. It is "absolutely clear," but still not bearable for human beings, "mortals": only fish and seals can live there. But aren't they mortal? In a sense, no, because they are not individual: they have the immortality of the *species* fish and seal. In much the same sense Keats addressed his nightingale as "Immortal Bird," emphasizing by contrast the weight of his own mortality as a conscious, particular being. After the ellipsis, Bishop shifts registers, as if the heaviness of the meditation had itself become as unbearable as the cold, dark water. She introduces an animal, a seal, into the poem and gives it particularity and identity. The tense changes to past and a little narrative of the encounter between the poet and the sea creature is given. The tone lightens, partly as a means of keeping reader interest fresh, and partly because there is something intrinsically comic about the spectacle of the poet singing "Baptist hymns" to an appreciative animal audience. But even here we find serious touches. For one thing, some folk legends consider seals to be the souls of drowned men; and apart from the presumably rousing Baptist hymns, "A Mighty Fortress Is Our God" also takes its place in the repertory. Instead of the gentle lamb, this hymn presents God as a medieval fortress, and we know Bishop dislikes armor and fortification. She establishes her kinship to the seal (as she had done earlier with the fisherman, for whom the animal may be a mythic replacement) by commenting that they are both believers "in total immersion." The humorous tone of this section allows for a pun at once comic and serious. Elizabeth Bishop was brought up as a Baptist, a denomination that baptizes by plunging the faithful under water. If one purpose of the baptismal rite is to symbolize death and resurrection, we can see how the idea of baptism fits into a poem that carefully develops symbolic affinities between the sea and death.

So much said, how are we to understand the poet's being a "believer in total immersion"? Of course many mythologies have associated the realm of the unconscious with the dark kingdom of the dead. The poet, in order to achieve full stature, must make an Orphic descent and return. To confront the revelation of the unconscious is like braving death itself, and small wonder if the prospect disturbs both poet and reader. At one moment, Bishop shows the seal as disappearing and then reemerging almost in the same spot, "with a sort of shrug / as if it were against his better judgment." But can a "mortal" do the same with impunity? Here Bishop repeats her characterization of the sea, "Cold dark deep and absolutely clear, / the clear gray icy water." But she does not seem able to maintain a steady gaze at this "element bearable to no mortal." Instead, she turns back to the shore to look at the firs, and the present tense and serious tone of the first part of the poem are resumed. She describes the firs as "bluish, associating with their shadows," as if they, too, might share her own awareness of the unconscious realm, the realm of shades. She says, "A million Christmas trees stand / waiting for Christmas." We know that Bishop stopped believing in the Christianity of her childhood, so we must read these lines ironically. The trees are not really waiting for Christmas; the natural world has no religious sense or consciousness at all. Besides, if Christmas did come to these trees, it would approach with an axe in its hand; they can be thought of as waiting for the joyous holiday in much the same sense as the fisherman waited for his ship to come in. In both cases, death is felt to be imminent.

The poem has moved from contemplation of a human being to contemplation of an animal and then to a plant. In the final movement, the gray funereal stones come into the foreground, made preternaturally clear and given an apparent motion by the water over them. "I have seen it over and over, the same sea, the same, / slightly, indifferently swinging above the stones," she says. The first-person singular subject pronoun has been used only three times before in the poem, in the anecdote of seeing the seal and singing to him: "I have seen . . . ," "so I used to sing . . . ," and "I also sang . . ." the lines go. The relationship between "seeing" and "singing" is emphasized in this passage, with its hypnotic repetitions and strong, rocking rhythms: "slightly, indifferently swinging above the stones, / icily free above the stones, / above the stones and then the world." Bishop sings here a lyric about the coldness of Nature and its indifference to human destiny; the stones of this little inlet in Nova Scotia come to symbolize the inhospitability of nature the world over. And yet, for all the bleakness of the prospect, the poet makes a magisterial song of her conclusion; she is able, like Orpheus, to set the stones dancing, through the visual illusion afforded by moving water, noted by the poet in phrases of rising and falling rhythm.

The next line brings in a personal pronoun not used earlier in the poem: "If you should dip your hand in, / your wrist would ache immediately." The speaker addresses someone other than herself here, for generalized self-reference up to now has been indicated by the impersonal pronoun "one." Another peculiarity about this section is its "shoulds" and "woulds." The seven lines are cast in a hypothetical mode, a summons for anyone listening to participate in an imaginative act: the probable effect of contact with the cove's symbolic water "would" be—and so forth. In context we must understand these sentences as addressed to the reader of the poem. A contemplation of the harshness of life, imminence of death, the indifference of Nature, and human loneliness has led the speaker to invent a listener, one capable of participating in the imaginative process. She apostrophizes "you," the reader, who may pass through the partial, symbolic baptism described. A hand is to be immersed, and then the water tasted. One writes with the hand, one speaks (or sings) with the tongue. Both members must undergo an ordeal that might be described as a visitation of the Pentecostal flame. The water "would first taste bitter, / then briny, then surely burn your tongue." At this point the poem shifts to the present tense and the first-person plural: "It is like what we imagine knowledge to be." Bishop has used first-person plural pronouns twice earlier in the poem, once with the old fisherman and once with the seal (in the objective case, "us.") Having addressed her readers and involved them in a hypothetical baptism, the poet feels confident to indicate a sense of shared imaginative power. She talked to the old man, sang hymns to the seal, and does something between talking and singing to us. Poet and reader unite in the kinship afforded by shared knowledge, a kind of knowledge that has, metaphorically, the qualities of the northern sea: "dark, salt, clear, moving, utterly free, / drawn from the cold hard mouth / of the world, derived from the rocky breasts. . . ." An undertone of sexuality can be heard in these lines, contact with an indifferent Nature presented as a form of total immersion but also as an encounter with death, "forever, flowing and drawn, and since / our knowledge is historical, flowing and flown."

From the image of flowing water, Bishop moves to the idea of passing time and brings in the notion of history. She takes a risk in introducing a new topic so near the end of the poem, but in fact, if we look back, we can find details "drawn" from several historical epochs. There is the primitive, archetypal figure of the fisherman, the medieval (figurative) "coats of mail," the Reformation hymn "A Mighty Fortress Is Our God," and nineteenth- and twentieth-century realia of all sorts. History is the record of change, and not only of political reality but also of human thought and culture: "our knowledge is historical." Hence even the insights reached in this poem are products of history, no less subject to flux than the natural world, "flowing and flown."

What Bishop presents here is a sort of negative Nativity, taking place among the primal elements and offering a form of knowledge that has none of the reassurance and permanence of the Incarnation. One is reminded of the moment in *Pericles* (Act III), when the storm-tossed ruler says to his infant daughter Marina, "Thou hast as chiding a Nativity / As fire, air, water, earth and heaven can make / To herald thee from the womb." Nature is unredeemed, and the only consolation Bishop offers is the moment of shared insight, in which poet and reader may feel a temporary kinship. That moment takes on resonance and power through lyric utterance, where the terror of change and death evoked by the first part of the poem is temporarily assuaged by a song *about* change and death in the poem's final section.

"At the Fishhouses" invites us to consider all forms of knowledge, including poetry, as provisional. If other poems of Bishop's reach different conclusions, they only confirm, by exemplifying, that provisionality. Earlier in *A Cold Spring* we find a series of poems in a more reassuring vein. To call the title poem, "Over 2000 Illustrations and a Complete Concordance" and "The Bight" reassuring poems needs qualification, however; Bishop almost always balances her affirmations with a current of doubt and counterassertion. "A Cold Spring" opens the volume, placing after its title the only epigraph Bishop ever used in her poetry, "Nothing is so beautiful as spring." A cheerful statement, and so is the

Hopkins sonnet (33, "Spring"), from which the line is drawn. "What is all this juice and all this joy? / A strain of the earth's sweet being in the beginning, / In Eden garden.— Have, get, before it cloy," Hopkins says. These elations contrast with the quieter tone of another Hopkins sonnet about spring (14), which is a meditation on coming late to religious truth. "See how Spring opens with disabling cold": Bishop borrows Hopkins's seasonal metaphor but adapts it to a different purpose. "A Cold Spring" uses religious allusions but only in order to treat a secular subject—the delayed arrival of sexual love, the "cold spring" in a human life.

Bishop's method is to portray this arrival in the changes that overtake a landscape. The poem's dedication ("to Jane Dewey. Maryland") prefigures that metaphor, placing the dedicatee's name next to her home state, where we assume Bishop is a guest. The very place name "Maryland" holds this same juxtaposition, a woman's name and the word "land." To underline the assimilation of dedicatee to geography, the poem brings in the second-person possessive pronoun four times, always in connection to some detail of the landscape. ". . . A grave, green dust / settled over your big and aimless hills." "Four deer practised leaping over your fences." ". . . Against your white front door, / the smallest moths, like Chinese fans, / flatten themselves." "And your shadowy pastures will be able to offer / these particular glowing tributes / every evening now throughout the summer." An estate in Maryland seems to take on attributes of the human body, and, what is more, the series of observations follows a progression in which hesitancy and resistance give way to acceptance and joy. The gradual warming trend of the delayed spring and consequent flowering of the landscape follow the same path.

Religious allusions in the poem belong to both great holidays of the Christian calendar. Easter comes in spring, of course, so we see the aptness of mentioning the redbud (or Judas tree, on which, according to legend, Jesus's betrayer hanged himself) and the dogwood, beams from which (according to legend) were used to make the cross. When the cardinal, that ecclesiastical bird, cracks the whip of his song, "the sleeper awoke." "Sleepers, Awake" is a well-known hymn, an injunction to the daughters of Jerusalem to go and greet the heavenly Bridegroom. But the awakening meant here is specifically a discovery of sexual pleasure. There is no real inconsistency in the fact that, when Bishop actually uses a personal pronoun for the personified landscape, she refers to this stretch of Maryland with the masculine possessive: ". . . and the sleeper awoke, / stretching miles of green limbs from the south. / In his cap the lilacs whitened, / then one day they fell like snow." The cold of the delayed spring has melted away, and the remainder of the poem portrays the warmth of summer, using the present tense and referring to details of the landscape as belonging to "you." Readers may pursue the process of finding metaphoric equivalents as far as seems appropriate.

A number of the religious allusions, as suggested earlier, have to do with Christmas, or the Nativity, which is less surprising when we consider that the Incarnation and Crucifixion are an inseparable theological pairing. "Sleepers, Awake," for example, is a hymn of the Advent season. Moreover, in March falls the feast of the Annunciation, and Bishop's epigraph tells us that Jane Dewey lives in Maryland.* In some sense, the annunciation made to her is both a sexual awakening and a kind of rebirth. In fact, the poem does describe a birth, though not of the Christ child: ". . . a calf was born. / The mother stopped lowing / and took a long time eating the afterbirth, / a wretched flag, / but the calf got up promptly / and seemed inclined to feel gay." Al-

---

*There is no way to know whether Bishop's studies of seventeenth-century poetry had brought to her attention Donne's "Upon the Annunciation and Passion Falling Upon One Day. 1608." If she knew the poem, different in subject and emphasis as it is, it may have helped shape the conceptual framework on which "A Cold Spring" is constructed.

though an animal birth is described, both parent and off-spring are humanized. Instead of using "heifer," Bishop calls her "the mother," and attributes human feelings to the calf. A summer of physical joy is ushered in, a new life to which metaphoric champagne toasts at the conclusion will be offered. In some sense this is both "Merry Easter" as well as "Merry Christmas." We recall that Easter was originally a pagan festival in honor of Eostre, goddess of the East, of dawn and spring, whose rites celebrated natural and human fertility. To the pagan survivals of Easter eggs and rabbits, Bishop adds the mother cow and her calf, summoning a new moon and fireflies as sacramental witnesses to this sexual awakening.

Bishop knew of course that the archetype of the Great Mother had its negative side, aspects that Christian mythology both incorporated and strove to transcend. The title "A Cold Spring" contains a possible pun; "spring" might also refer to a source of water, which Bishop can describe as "drawn from the cold hard mouth / of the world, derived from the rocky breasts." If the earth, or Nature, is a nurturing mother, it can also be felt as indifferent to human suffering and death; and it is where we are finally buried, reabsorbed into brute matter. Reflections like these perhaps influence Bishop's insistence on "the Tomb, the Pit, the Sepulcher" in "Over 2000 Illustrations and a Complete Concordance," which follows directly after "A Cold Spring." The donnée of the poem is simple: two heavy books are, figuratively, weighed and compared, an old illustrated Bible and the "book" of "our travels." Next to the Bible, with its "serious, engravable" story and Concordance (a pun is intended), the poet's unsystematic tourism seems negligible. Instead of sacred history, with its structure of redemption from death, the poet has only a discordant miscellany to offer. Beginning with the line "Entering the Narrows at St. Johns," Bishop writes a brief summary of her travels, a catalogue of disparate, random scenes, some of them beautiful:

"at Volubilis, there were beautiful poppies"; "in Dingle harbor a golden length of evening . . ." the poem elaborates. On
first reading we might see in the travelogue nothing more
telling than an evening's slide show in Kodachrome. But
toward the end she says, "It was somewhere near there / I
saw what frightened me most of all . . ." a statement that
sends us back to the list of memories in order to find what in
it is sinister or frightening. The figure of the dead man in
Mexico, who "lay in a blue arcade" is terrible enough, but
what else? The deserted ruin at Volubilis, with its poppies
"splitting the mosaics" could serve as a standard emblem for
the destructions of time. And the fact of the imminent birth
of the duchess's child? Presumably, a joyous event; except
that the travelers are told about it during a very civilized
tea—whereupon the travelogue moves directly to Marrakesh
and its brothels, with prostitutes who "balanced their tea-
trays on their heads." The astute montage here draws us up
short before a worldwide condition of social inequity and
servitude. The women of Marrakesh may serve tea to who-
ever can pay for it, but they will never be allowed, like the
duchess, to have and raise a child. Nativity is denied to them.

Finally it is the universal absence of religious sanctions and
social benevolence in modern life that is so frightening to
Bishop. Christianity persists in a few historical vestiges—in
names like Saint Johns or Saint Peter's, the central edifice of
Roman Catholicism, its collegians "crisscrossing the great
square with black, like ants" (not a pleasing image). The
travelogue concludes at a nameless Moslem shrine out in a
"pink desert," where another holy grave, the tomb of a
prophet, proves to contain nothing but dust, not even the
prophet's remains. The tomb is a marble trough, "yellowed /
as scattered cattle teeth." Whether or not the reader is reminded of the mother and her calf in the previous poem, the
message is clear: time destroys bodies and even dismantles
the structures of religion.

This detailed preamble leads to a concluding meditation on

the poet's regret at her lack of faith, her inability to see a meaningful pattern in experience. The life of travel without religious faith is a miscellany, "Everything only connected by 'and' and 'and.'" The three consecutive *and*s reverberate with deafening insistence. The poet has no alternative but to reopen the Bible and examine the sacred story once again. She looks at a picture of the stable in Bethlehem and wishes she could witness, in whatever sense, the Nativity. She is like the Hardy of "The Oxen," who reflects on Christmas Eve that, if someone told him the animals were kneeling in a barn nearby (if the Nativity were being reenacted), "I should go with him through the gloom, / Hoping it might be so." For her part, Bishop allows herself to imagine and describe, in lines of great splendor, the illustrated divine birth:

> —the dark ajar, the rocks breaking with light,
> an undisturbed, unbreathing flame,
> colorless, sparkless, freely fed on straw,
> and, lulled within, a family of pets. . . .

Presumably these pets would include cattle or oxen for the moment turning aside from their trough (recall the "marble trough" above) and kneeling before the child sent to save the world. If we could have seen this, she says, we could have "looked and looked our infant sight away." In short, we could have given up mere seeing in favor of vision. As David Kalstone (in *Five Temperaments*) has pointed out, "infant" keeps its root meaning here of *infans,* or "speechless." Next to the kind of vision offered by the Nativity, the seeing we have in the secular world is one without anything to say, "speechless," infantile.

Two factors temper the bleakness of this estimate of the unbeliever's situation. The travelogue, for all its miscellany, injustice, and terror, stumbles on moments of delight—the Saint Johns goats, with their "touching bleat," "leaping up the cliffs / among the fog-soaked weeds and butter-and-eggs," for example. Perhaps these and other moments can serve as humble compensations for the missing Holy Family and its "pets." Moreover, Bishop does actually compose a verbal picture of the Nativity. The lines cited above, with their beautifully imagined light and phrasing, themselves leave the door of darkness ajar and amount to a kind of vision it would be sullen to dismiss, even should the reader find the "negative Nativity" at the conclusion of "At the Fishhouses" more compelling still. Both passages are built out of elemental imagery, but the Nova Scotian landscape is an actual scene. The conclusion to "Over 2000 Illustrations" shows that Bishop has managed a second, *imaginary* Epiphany—and has made poetry of it. Bishop reminds one here of the Stevens of *Notes Toward a Supreme Fiction*. Having imagined, in the poem, an angel that wings upward to the topmost pinnacle of blissful vision, Stevens asks himself: "Is it he or I that experience this?" Even subject–verb agreement tells us that the poet himself has appropriated the angelic vision, so that Stevens can conclude, "there is a time / In which majesty is a mirror of the self." He means the nonhistorical "time" of poetic vision, which fosters secular as well as religious epiphanies. For Bishop, as for the Stevens of *Notes*, poetry offers the only available alternative to divine revelation.

After an animal birth and then the birth of the Christ Child, in "The Bight" Bishop turns to her own birthday. The series cannot be accidental, and I think we are to understand the birthday recorded in "The Bight" as the "nativity" of the artist. In order to treat it fully, however, we must first move forward to *Questions of Travel,* the collection published after *A Cold Spring.* The volume was unusual in that it included, apart from some nineteen poems, an autobiographical short story, "In the Village." Bishop probably relied on Lowell's *Life Studies* as her most immediate precedent. Lowell's "91 Revere Street" in that volume is presented as a nonfiction memoir, but studies have shown that a good deal of invented material went into its composition. "In the Village" is presented as a work of fiction, but my estimate is that, allowing for artistic heightening, the events recorded all happened to Bishop during one summer of her childhood. It is a story of emotional shock and the effect of that shock on the developing psyche of a child, in this case, a child who grew up to become an artist.

The central metaphor in the story is built around the scream that broke from the narrator's mother at a moment of crisis. We are made to understand how this scream led, first, to a habit of extreme perceptual attentiveness in the child and then to the adult Bishop's compensatory effort to make durable artifacts from that habit of attention. Consider the opening paragraph of the story, written in the present tense:

> A scream, the echo of a scream, hangs over that Nova Scotian village. No one hears it; it hangs there forever, a slight stain in those pure blue skies, skies that travellers compare to those of Switzerland, too dark, too blue, so that they seem to keep on darkening a little more around the horizon—or is it around the rims of the eyes?—the color of the cloud of bloom on the elm trees, the violet on the fields of oats; something darkening over the woods and waters as well as the sky. The scream hangs like that, unheard, in memory—in the past, in the present, and those years between. It was not even loud to begin with, perhaps. It just came there to live forever—not loud, just alive forever. Its pitch would be the pitch of my village. Flick the lightning rod on top of the church steeple with your fingernail and you will hear it.

The "forever" of this paragraph, repeated twice, belongs to the hyperbole of art or, we may say, the *eternity* of art, which can transform a lightning flash of emotion into something unshakable and permanent. Here a fleeting sound is magicked into a visual particular: the "echo of a scream" becomes a "stain" in the "pure blue skies." (Bishop may have had in mind Siqueiros's well-known painting *The Echo of a Scream*, which shows a child sitting on a pile of rubble in a war-torn landscape. The child is crying, and an image of his face, much enlarged, hovers over him like a terrifying visual echo.)

The scream, which occurs during a dress-fitting for the child narrator's mother, would have seemed less momentous if it had not been the culmination of an already extreme psychological conflict. The mother, not long out of a sanatorium where she has been recuperating from a nervous collapse after the death of her husband, is being fitted for her first dress in colors—she is trying to end, if only by external signs, the period of mourning. The seamstress cuts her dress from a purple material. Overheard during the fitting are sounds coming from a nearby blacksmith's shop. The bell-like note (*"clang"*) of the blacksmith's hammer and forge is repeated several times, described as "The pure note: pure and angelic." Then suddenly, "The dress was all wrong. She screamed. The child vanishes." The effort to give up mourning has been too great; the mother has not recovered.

Frightened by the scream, the child goes off to visit Nate, the blacksmith, and she seems to draw some kind of reassurance from him and his skillful labor. We follow the child on other errands, told in the present tense, as the story unfolds luminous descriptions of the village, its houses, people, animals—descriptions wonderful in their detail, inventiveness, and sharp, bright coloration. When the dramatic narrative resumes some time later, it is clear that the mother's condition has not improved; nor does she ever put aside mourning in favor of her new dress. One night a nearby barn burns down. For whatever reason, this event brings on another crisis for the mother. (There is a remote suggestion that she may have set the fire herself.) In any case, the mother has to return to the sanatorium for treatment, leaving the child with her grandparents. Without directly labeling emotions, the narrator lets us feel the enormity of the event and its psychological consequences.

"In the Village" shows us why and how Bishop became a poet. A Venus figure, her mother, comes to be redeemed by a sort of Vulcan, the blacksmith (understood as a symbol of the artist). Bishop's fable has both an auditory and a visual aspect. If the scream in the story's opening paragraph was transposed into a stain in the skies of the village, it also fuses with the loud *clang* of the blacksmith's hammer and forge, the "pure, angelic note." It may help to recall Dickinson's poem "Dare you see a Soul *at the White Heat?*" to read this allegory. The concluding lines remind us that, "Least Village has its Blacksmith / Whose Anvil's even ring / Stands symbol for the finer Forge / That soundless tugs—within— / Refining these impatient Ores / With Hammer, and with Blaze / Until the Designated Light '/ Repudiate the Forge—." Bishop has devised a plausible and resonant allegory for the artist as a maker. Also, remembering the importance of the Nativity story for Bishop, we can understand why she named her blacksmith Nate; she wants to tell the story of the birth of an artist, metaphorically, the child of Venus and Vulcan.

And what kind of poet will she be? The adjective *purple,* since at least the time of Horace, has been used (in the phrase "purple patch") to characterize writing that is highly wrought, brilliantly colored, and especially ingenious. If Bishop has often been criticized as too descriptive, too brilliantly visual, "In the Village" helps account for the trait. When the child-narrator sees the purple dress at the seamstress's, she says, "Oh, look away before it moves or makes a sound; before it echoes, echoes, what it has heard!" A color is being assimilated to a sound, in this case, a sound bearing a burden of extreme tension. Bishop's visual particulars, in part, are indicators of great emotional stress. Tennyson anticipates this use of brilliant imagery as a sign of psychological tension in both "Mariana" and *Maud,* and some of Virginia Woolf's novels might be instanced as well. In fact, psychologists have noted that hysteria and even schizophrenia sometimes show themselves in the form of heightened visual acuity, an absorption in the particularity of random objects. That is the negative side of the personality trait. But we can understand it in another way: if Bishop dwells at length on the forms and colors of the world, part of the effort embodies a desire to make the world go from black and white into color, in short, to *bring the world out of mourning* (or out from under the sway of Calvinist judgment), as her mother never managed to do. Near the end of the story, when her grand-mother sends presents to the sanatorium, the child notices that she addresses them in purple ink. To save the appear-ances of the world is an effort to save a life, to restore it to happiness and well-being. (I notice, too, that the book-jacket design for *Questions of Travel* showed an old map of the Western Hemisphere, with the land masses printed in purple against a sea-green background.)

If the story's visual aspect centers around the mother-Venus figure, the auditory aspect is connected to the black-smith Nate and contributes a series of meanings just as tell-ing. Apart from the insistent repetition of the sound of Nate's hammer, several other *clang*s ring throughout the story: the soft sound of cowbells when the child drives a herd to pas-ture; a little bell on the door of the sweetshop where she is sent by her mother; and finally the church bell that rings an alarm when the barn burns down. Any others? It is possible that Bishop may have recalled a comparable series of bells in Lowell's long poem *The Mills of the Kavanaughs*—church bell, doorbell, bell on a snowplow, and then (overheard by the widow narrator), her dead husband's mother, who "waits for us, / And types, until the clattering tin bell / Upon her room-large table tolls for us." Apparently the mother-in-law is typing a memoir or novel that she means to sell in order to solve the Kavanaughs' money problems. In the days before our relatively silent computers, manual typewriters (like the Smith-Corona) tolled the approach of the right-hand margin at the end of every typed line, which might be felt as a kind of striking of the measure. Can Bishop have thought of her machine as a poetic equivalent to Nate's forge? The conclusion of the story brings in one more metaphoric bell, the bell buoy, which of course floats out in the sea, the realm of engulfment and death, and helps prevent shipwrecks. Here is Bishop:

> *Clang.*
> It sounds like a bell buoy out at sea.
> It is the elements speaking: earth, air, fire, water.
> All those other things—clothes, crumbling postcards, broken china; things damaged and lost, sickened or destroyed; even the frail almost-lost scream—are they too frail for us to hear their voices long, too mortal?
> Nate!
> Oh, beautiful sound, strike again!

The metaphoric marine setting and the invocation of the primal elements remind us of the conclusions to "At the Fishhouses" and "Over 2000 Ilustrations and a Complete Concordance," two earlier versions of the Nativity. The bell tolling here, however, is neither funeral bell nor Christmas bell, but the life-saving clangor, musical and workmanly, of artistic creation, whose end is, in Dickinson's phrase, the "Designated Light."

"In the Village" is an extended prose treatment of a theme handled earlier in the poem "The Bight," which follows directly after "A Cold Spring" and "Over 2000 Illustrations." After the depiction of an animal and divine birth, Bishop turns to the birth of an artist, and the poem is written, the poet tells us, "On my birthday." This poem is seldom discussed in detail, probably because the abundance of visual notation in it resists interpretation. Once again we may admire the brilliance and aptness of the description, but there is no reason to stop there. For the poem takes on resonance as soon as we begin to see it as a metaphor for writing.

In Bishop's allegorical system, the "white marl" stands for the white page, the "ocher dredge" for the effort to reach down into the unconscious and draw up material to be transformed into poetry (recall a similar effort exerted by dry land in "The Map"). The scene of the poem, a small harbor in

Key West, is suffused with an understated emotional tension, tonally akin to the scream of "In the Village." We gather that there has been a recent storm in this tranquil seascape. Private personal dramas are hinted at in the phrase, "torn-open, un-answered letters." But at the level of allegory these may stand in for failed drafts of a poem. "Letters" are made to sort in a punning fashion with Baudelaire's doctrine of *correspon-dances*, or, as it is sometimes called, "synaesthesia," the link-ing of the terms of one kind of sensory perception to those of another ("loud colors," "sweet sounds," and so forth). The prevailing aura of anxiety is made to glint and glance off sharp objects in the scene. Pelicans are "like pickaxes" (re-minding us of the Greek root for their name, *pelekus*, an axe). The black and white man-o'-war birds "open their tails like scissors." (In fact, they may actually be, at the level of alle-gory, scissors used to cut and rearrange drafts of a poem.) There are shark tails hung up to dry—nor is any other, more benign fish species mentioned. The sharks, at least—caught, killed, and dismembered—have been beaten, metaphor-ically, into "plowshares," an item in the "Chinese restaurant trade."

Readers may carry the process of allegorical matching-up as far as seems appropriate. * The pilings described as "dry as matches" could suggest more than the bare simile itself does,

---

*After this essay was written, an article by David Kalstone appeared (*Grand Street,* vol. 4, no. 4, p. 176), in which part of a letter from Bishop to Lowell was quoted, as follows:

> "The water looks like blue gas—the harbor is always a mess here, junky little boats all piled up, some hung with sponges and always a few half sunk or splintered up from the most recent hurricane—it reminds me a little of my desk."

I hope my allegorical reading of "The Bight" is convincing without this external evidence, but I offer this much here to those readers who might deny that Bishop intended more than one level of meaning in her ostensi-bly "realistic" poems.

for example, particularly if the writer was in the habit of smoking—as we know she was from a poem written much later, "12 O'Clock News." (That poem of course is a much more explicit allegory of the writer's desk and helps us discover in the earlier, less explicit "The Bight" some of the metaphoric energies at work.) To remark the pun in Bishop's phrase "impalpable drafts" should suffice, for present purposes, to sum up the general strategy of "The Bight," itself a punning title perfectly in accord with the sharp, tearing paraphernalia in the poem and with the ocher dredge's "jawful of dripping marl." Whether or not the poem was actually written on Bishop's birthday matters less than that it was written on the *poem's* birthday. This particular nativity has come as a difficult birth, perhaps, but also as some kind of triumph.

To register the full import of the final sentence, "All the untidy activity continues, / awful but cheerful," we should return to "In the Village." At one point the child narrator describes the scene around the barn on the morning after it was burned: "There are people still standing around, some of them the men who got up in the night to go to the river. Everyone seems quite cheerful there, too, but the smell of burned hay is awful, sickening." In the story, the sequence went "cheerful . . . but . . . awful"; in the poem Bishop puts matters the other way, reversing the emphasis. (There has already been sounded a grim note in the rhyme "jawful" and "awful.") The rhythm of the brief last line, incidentally, approximates the classical foot called "adonic," long-short-short-long-long. This is the foot used as the last line of the Greek and Latin sapphic stanza, for example. For Bishop, although life is terrible and barbaric, and the effort to capture it in poetry hazardous also, the proper response is neither despair nor rage but a concerted effort to be, as she says, "gay," like the newborn calf in "A Cold Spring." We remember that the art of the troubadours, the Provençal love poets, was known as the *"Gai Saber,"* the Gay Science. In art, that *"saber"* asks the poet to transform private suffering into a poetry of delight and brilliance, the surface of which refers to another order of meaning hidden below. "The Bight," as a little fable of poetic composition, leaves us with Bishop's motto for her "new, tender, quick" art and her ABC of existence: Awful, yes. But, also, Cheerful. It is vibrant but delicate teaching—and small wonder, considering the vulnerability of the first student to whom the lesson is addressed. Small wonder, too, that so many readers have been willing to go to school with her in this and other poems, equipped as these are with brilliant maps of experience and a discourse of self-examination that seems less like instruction than the discovery of new worlds. *

*One of the new worlds discovered by Elizabeth Bishop was, of course, the country of Brazil. It is interesting to note that her Time-Life nonfiction book about Brazil begins with the story of a birth—and ensuing hazards attending on it. What's more, two Nativity poems were added to Bishop's *Complete Poems* during her stay in South America. One is a translation from the Portuguese of João Cabral de Melo Neto, titled "The Death and Life of a Severino, A Pernambuco Christmas Play, 1954–1955." The final section is titled "A Child Has Just Been Born," and it begins, "All heaven and earth / are singing in his praise." And finally there is the trenchant and touching Epiphany poem called "Twelfth Morning; *or* What You Will."

13

God's Spies: Elizabeth Bishop and John Hollander

Travel and imprisonment are complementary conditions, and both have been recurrent themes in Elizabeth Bishop's writing. "In Prison," an early prose work, begins: "I can scarcely wait for the day of my imprisonment." It goes on to meditate ad lib on the respective advantages of life on the right and wrong side of the bars—reversing our notions about which is which. The narrator argues, with a certain logic, in favor of choosing prison, of choosing Necessity. Among the several benefits that should accrue is the ability to see with extraordinary clarity, even if the sight is only a brick wall or a cobbled courtyard at sunset. The narrator also plans to scribble messages on the wall: "brief, suggestive, anguished, but full of the lights of revelation." The story has many resonances, but certainly, as an allegory, it outlines, with much charm and point, the condition of the writer— who ought, on this view, not hesitate when Lear says, "Come, let's away to prison. . . . And take upon's the mystery of things, / As if we were God's spies."

*Geography III** comes nominally under the travel rubric, but it is equally concerned with imprisonment, voluntary and involuntary. The book is accurately summed up by the phrase above: "brief, suggestive, anguished, but full of the

*Farrar, Straus and Giroux, 1976.

lights of revelation." Its special qualities include a perfected transparence of expression, warmth of tone, and a singular blend of sadness and good humor, of pain and acceptance—a radiant patience few people ever achieve and fewer writers ever successfully render. The poems are works of philo- sophic beauty and calm, illuminated by that "laughter in the soul" that belongs to the best part of the comic genius.

Two earlier collections had titles suggesting travel; hence *Geography III,* with the added resonance of lessons learned. The title poem of *Questions of Travel* succinctly presents the polarity that operates in so much of Bishop's writing:

> *"Is it lack of imagination that makes us come*
> *to imagined places, not just stay at home?*
>
> *Or could Pascal have been not entirely right*
> *about just sitting quietly in one's room?*
>
> *Continent, city, country, society:*
> *the choice is never wide and never free."*

In the new book the narrator of "Crusoe" looks back not to his travels but to the period when he was marooned on a small island (never identified, but apparently one of the Ga- lápagos). The narrator is not, by the way, Defoe's character; he is used rather as an archetype. Most of the poem is taken up with the terms—physical, emotional, and philosophical— of Crusoe's confinement. He describes his volcanic island as "a sort of cloud-dump," with beaches "all lava, variegated, / black, red, and white, and gray." He recounts the limited daily round of his existence and alludes with irony to his "is- land industries," the smallest of which is "a miserable philos- ophy." Even that doesn't always avail:

> I often gave way to self-pity.
> "Do I deserve this? I suppose I must.
> I wouldn't be here otherwise. Was there

a moment when I actually chose this?
I don't remember but there could have been."

Crusoe concludes that "'Pity should begin at home.' So the more / pity I felt, the more I felt at home."

A carefully maintained state of bemused desperation seems to help as well. Crusoe names one of his little volcanoes *"Mont d'Espoir* or Mount Despair." He quotes Wordsworth on "That inward eye, which is the bliss of . . ." but he can't remember the word "solitude," perhaps because the fact of it is already unbearable. He might, just as appositely, have echoed Byron's Prisoner of Chillon, who "learned to love despair," as well as his fellow inmate creatures—birds, mice, spiders. Crusoe is sometimes able to beguile his time by watching the island's goats, gulls, turtles, and tree-snails; then Friday arrives, the perfect companion in every way but one. The Prison of Chillon said he regained his freedom with a sigh; and Bishop's Crusoe, rescued, says, "Now I live here, another island, / that doesn't seem like one, but who decides? . . . The living soul has dribbled away." Has he gained or lost? In fact, the poem splendidly straddles the question, balancing off exile, hardship, solitude, and vision against homecoming, comfort, boredom, and memory. On his island Crusoe seems to have agreed with the Coleridge of "This Lime Tree Bower, My Prison," who says, "No waste so vacant, but may well employ / Each faculty of sense, and keep the heart / Awake to Love and Beauty!" Repatriated, Crusoe is probably mistaken in believing that "the living soul has dribbled away," but certainly its function has changed, and his poem is the proof. The soul that sees imaginatively has been replaced by the soul that remembers imaginatively and makes art.

"In the Waiting Room" is another poem about imprisonment, not in space but in time and in anatomy, which has traditionally been a good half of destiny. More precisely, the poem recounts a little girl's terrifying discovery that she lives in time, has an identity, and that part of her identity depends on the fact that she will eventually grow up to be a woman, like her Aunt Consuelo. (Bishop dealt with similar moments of crisis in children's lives in the stories of "Gwendolyn" and "In the Village"; it must have been material of this kind that interested her, as well, in translating *The Diary of "Helena Morley,"* written by a young Brazilian girl in the early part of this century.) The little girl of "In the Waiting Room" is obviously based on the author—several details seem to be autobiographical, and indeed the very factuality of the poem is unusual. We are given the date when the incident takes place, and told that the narrator's seventh birthday is three days off. The *National Geographic* she looks through is dated February 1918, and the description of its pictures is remarkably detailed:

> Babies with pointed heads
> wound round and round with string;
> black, naked women with necks
> wound round and round with wire
> like the necks of light bulbs.
> Their breasts were horrifying.

The type of picture essay is familiar; but it is not to be found in the February 1918 *National Geographic*. Anyone checking to see whether Miss Bishop's aunt was named Consuelo probably ought to be prepared for a similar thwarting of curiosity. (A good reminder that poems are imaginative fictions; the rest is not quite literature.) If the facts are "wrong," why did Bishop make such a point of them in the poem? I think they must be there to emphasize the little girl's discovery that she has an identity, one that must be lived in time. If the discovery of her eventual womanhood is terrifying, there may still be mitigating considerations; possibly Aunt Consuelo (whose name means "consolation") stands as a reminder of some kind of compensatory knowledge; this poem doesn't state what that might be, but the other poems begin to.

One of the most beautiful—and mysterious—poems in the collection is "The Moose." Its opening sentence, running for 36 lines, describes the Nova Scotian landscape familiar from earlier Bishop. The sentence moves from the general to the ever more particular, and eventually we realize that it coincides with the steady progress and approach of a bus; when the bus stops to collect a "lone traveller" (the narrator), the sentence stops too. Then,

> Goodbye to the elms,
> to the farm, to the dog.
> The bus starts. The light
> grows richer; the fog,
> shifting, salty, thin,
> comes closing in.
>
> Its cold, round crystals
> form and slide and settle
> in the white hens' feathers,
> in gray glazed cabbages,
> on the cabbage roses
> and lupins like apostles. . . .

(Passages like this one remind us that, as Richard Wilbur has said, description is "an elaborate and enchanted form of naming.") After nightfall the traveler's attention is drawn to the conversation of some elderly passengers in the rear of the bus. Enlarged by darkness and anonymity, these seem to be "Grandparents' voices / uninterruptedly / talking, in Eternity." Memories arise of the traveler's own grandparents, presumably dead, left behind in time and space. At the sudden appearance of a moose, the bus driver brakes and stops; the passengers stare at the strange apparition. It is a confrontation between the human and nonhuman; the machine and nature; the present and the past. Then, the bus drives on in "a dim / smell of moose, an acrid / smell of gasoline."

In "The End of March" a walk in cold weather along a

Massachusetts beach becomes the occasion for another meditation on solitude within narrow confines. The poet sees a
green shingled house, "my proto-dream-house," and says,

> I'd like to retire there and do *nothing*
> or nothing much, forever, in two bare rooms:
> look through binoculars, read boring books, . . .
> and foggy days,
> watch the droplets slipping, heavy with light.

Predictably, she and her companions never reach the house;
in any case, she recognizes the dream as unrealizable. The
poem avoids ending on a note of dejection, however. The
sun appears for a few moments, bringing out the several colors of the beach pebbles; and the poet charmingly imagines
the sun as a lion "who perhaps had batted a kite out of the sky
to play with." The fanciful dream is hauled down; the poet is
restored to the world.

In "Poem" Bishop examines a small painting by her "Un-
cle George," no doubt the same person as the painter who
did the "Large Bad Picture" in her first book. The poignancy
of this subject, revisited after more than thirty years, draws
much of its force from a similar juxtaposition within the
poem. The painted scene, contemplated at length, is recognized by the poet as a place remembered from childhood. As
one reads the poem, several entities are present: the earlier
"Large Bad Picture"; this second painting; the poet's memory of the actual landscape depicted; and now the new poem
being written about the painting and its subject. When
Bishop speaks of "shared vision" (revising her term, then, to
the unnecessarily modest "look"), a rainbow of relationships
unfolds. A little miracle of consciousness unites painter, poet,
and reader in the "shared vision" of a landscape:

> Life and the memory of it cramped,
> dim, on a piece of Bristol board,

dim, but how live, how touching in detail
—the little that we get for free,
the little of our earthly trust. Not much.
About the size of our abidance
along with theirs: the munching cows,
the iris, crisp and shivering, the water
still standing from spring freshets,
the yet-to-be-dismantled elms, the geese.

Only the "Not much" seems inaccurate; in this "Poem"
and in Bishop's others there seems to be a special dispensa-
tion, where sentences are suspended in an atmosphere of freedom and affection—and that is a good deal.

PRISON might be one place for poets to become "God's
spies," but presumably they could do as well out in the field
as "secret agents," up to their elbows in life and work. John
Hollander's *Reflections on Espionage** is an extended metaphorical treatment of a special sort of conspiracy—"Us," the
milieu of art, vision, understanding, the "altogether inconve-
nient little republic" of letters, against "Them," the philis-
tines. Beginning with this neat analogy for the marginal state
of contemporary poets, Hollander's long poem establishes
several more equivalences: the verse is presented as a series of
encoded messages, identified by month and day, and trans-
mitted to other agents or to a "control" (who may be understood as a sympathetic critic). The "Work" undertaken by
Hollander's group of master spies is nothing less than the
writing of the poetry of our own day; and it is all done under
the direction of a top-flight commander styled "Lyrebird,"
viz., Apollo or the Muse.

The poem's agent-narrator, code name "Cupcake," is, I
assume, based on Hollander himself, and I believe "real life"
prototypes for most of the other agents could be found. (The

*Atheneum, 1976.

temptation is to guess who these might be; but, apart from the danger of putting one's foot in one's mouth, there is, again, the consideration that poems should be judged primarily as imaginative fictions.)

What Cupcake and his creator have in common is that they both seem to know everything. John Hollander holds, surely, the Monsieur Teste chair in American letters. His earlier poetry and criticism frequently and usefully allude to many kinds of learning—scientific, historical, musical—when these might throw light on the issues under consideration. *Vision and Resonance,* his study of poetry as a sonic and visual entity, is the most informative and infectiously interesting treatise to date on that subject. And Hollander's learning serves him well in his poetry, as both stimulus and substance. So often when we read poetry we feel we are sharing the life of perhaps heartening but elementary minds; I always welcome any occasion to listen to poetry that is rich in verifiable truths as well as in vatic ones—especially when, as in Hollander's case, it's all done with agility and good humor.

Amusement will probably be most readers' first reaction to Hollander's parodic spy thriller, but I doubt it will be the last. The humor and wit so apparent in these pages suggest that the poet is dealing with matters too important to be presented with unrelieved earnestness, too urgent to risk leaving the reader in the detachment of pity or polite toleration. Cupcake's modest, jaunty transmissions, his simple faith in the Work, and his quietly stated doubts about his own value to it, or its overall significance, activate our sympathies without exacting them:

> . . . I ask for nothing
> More than to do the work, to be able
> To work. It is not given us to complete
> It; neither are we free to desist from it.
>   [9/13]

For nine months we observe Cupcake at the Work, listen to his characterization of other agents, and weigh his own ratiocinative or imaginative meditations, all of them cast in hendecasyllabic lines (or code "grids") as in the above sample. Some of Cupcake's most interesting reflections turn around the relationship between espionage (poetry) and the agent's "cover" (his ostensible profession), since in our day most poets must make their living by doing something besides writing poetry (teaching, for example, as in Hollander's case). Cupcake raises, and wisely does not settle, many pointed questions on this subject. There are, besides, other issues to confront. During the nine-month period recorded, something seems to be gestating; this proves to be Cupcake's death or rather his "termination," the order for it coming down from Lyrebird. No definite reason for the "termination" is given—but it is implicit. When Hollander's muse stops being stimulated by the persona of "Cupcake," it's time to drop him and for the book to end. Of course, there may be more to it than that, for *Reflections on Espionage* is a richly textured work, multilayered, and evocative of meanings leading in several directions.

Among Cupcake's concerns some can be deciphered as visionary; and the terms he uses in talking about them remind us of Mallarmé and Stevens. Anyone who knows modern poetry will almost reflexively decode Cupcake's aspirations toward a final Cipher as the Supreme Fiction Stevens made notes toward, or, again, as the final book Mallarmé asserted the world was destined to become. Mallarmé appears to be Hollander's most telling precursor in French (though possibly the same could be said for any American poet who has read him; Mallarmé is, I think, the quintessential modern poet). In Hollander's poem "Aristotle to Phyllis" (from *Movie-Going*) there are, as he has pointed out, several lines from Mallarmé's "Brise marine" buried in the text as English sonic approximations—the *mots d'heures gousse rames* word-game, but in reverse. Again, in section V of his *Visions from the Ramble,* Hollander rings changes on the famous "Ces nymphes, je les veux perpétuer," which opens *L'Après-midi d'un faune:* "These nymphs the winter would perpetuate, Secure in their twigs. . . ."

In the present volume, the theme of the night-long poetic vigil at the heart of "Brise marine" and "Don du poème" is rendered by Cupcake in his 4/18 transmission to agent Image as follows: "long stretches of intensity / Without the quickening excitement, which comes / With decipherment, and then nausea at dawn. . . . / It is as if one had been drained of something / Like light." And the Mallarmean (or Stevensian) longing for a final fusion of world and text takes this form in Hollander:

> To come upon the final Cipher,
> . . . .
> . . . . one would come to discern
> The world—even the innocent, unworking
> World—in it, would somehow walk in its rhythms
> Of transposition, in its modes of shifting.
> . . . .
> A poem whose form was of the world itself.
>
> [5/10]

(Notice here that when Cupcake needs a metaphor for his cipher, he arrives at "poem," much as a mirror image, reflected again, restores left to left and right to right. Reflections indeed.)

Cupcake then, among recent American voices, seems to have the clearest sense of the Mallarmean imagination. And Mallarmé's notion of the *azur* he seems very much at home with. The most characteristic Hollander moment has always seemed to be one captured in an environment at high altitudes and low temperatures, with cloudless, ultramarine skies. Canto X from *The Head of the Bed* and "Mount Blank" from *Tales Told of the Fathers* spring to mind as examples. In such an atmosphere, the clear-eyed intellect of a "Cupcake" sees what it is best skilled to describe:

> . . . The weather
> Is dry and very cold, and the reception
> Should be better in this clear, cornflower-blue
> Evening sky, low winds humming through icy
> Wires above clusters of starlings crackling—
>
> [1/18]

Among English poets probably the most important for Hollander is Ben Jonson. Certainly Jonson has had few critics as sympathetic as Hollander. The two are like in their complete possession of poetic tradition; and Hollander also seems to share Jonson's healthy attitude toward the classics, which the English poet termed "Guides, not Commanders." It may be, too, that the whole encoding conceit in *Reflections* is an allusion to Jonson's notoriously reasonable method of composition: poems were written "first in prose, for so his master Cambden had Learned him." Or, as Cupcake puts it, "a pressing message / Remains, uncoded in its naked plain on / The desk by one's left hand. . . ." I single out one more hidden allusion in the book's footnote to transmission 1/27: "These 'refrains' were enciphered simply as 'turn' after the first one." This may remind the reader of Jonson's ode to Cary and Morison, with its strophes labeled "The Turne," "The Counterturne," and "The Stand," a poem Hollander has written about with great affection. The three labels already figured in a line from the lovely poem "The Sundial," collected in Hollander's first book.

In the twentieth century the poet most resembling Jonson is Auden; and some of the typical concerns of both—reasonableness, loyalty, and an interest in writing in many different poetic genres—have been inherited by Hollander. The association between Hollander and Auden was personal as well as literary, of course; and here I will quote the first but one of Cupcake's transmissions, which details the death of "Steampump," an agent unquestionably based on Auden:

> Steampump is gone. He died quietly in his
> Hotel room and his sleep. His cover people

Attended to everything. What had to
Be burned was burned. He taught me, as you surely
Know, all that I know;

[1/15]

I hazard that one of the germinating impulses for *Reflections* was a desire to present, in code, a portrait of what remains of Auden's influence in American poetry. The "covers" that I can identify all seem to have at least a tenuous relationship to Auden, either as poets he chose for the Yale Series, or as his friends, his disciples, or disciples of his disciples. This group, mutatis mutandis, is a fair equivalent for the celebrated Tribe of Ben that accounts for most of the important early seventeenth-century poetry in England after Jonson's death. Perhaps this parallel struck Hollander.

The assertion of a real—though not pious—sense of community in Hollander's rendering of the present milieu of poetry is one of the book's most attractive features. He allows us to see how poets, at least some of them, must view each other's work and careers—not as a mad, competitive scramble, but as a kind of teamwork (see, for example, Cupcake's enthusiastic reaction to agent Image's "Project Alphabet"). The world limned out in this book has broader implications than its immediate reference, of course. It could serve as a model for an imaginative community on any scale, one whose members were all respectfully conscious of the others' lives, work, and "signifying" capacity. In such a utopia, citizens specifically designated as poets might vanish. Cupcake seems to be aware of the possibility: "as if the whole world perhaps were / At the work? What then? Why then there would be no / Need of it." But we are far away from that, I think. A book like *Reflections on Espionage* is still very necessary, nor could anyone but a poet have written it.

14

Hart Crane's "Atlantis"

Commentators have not been surprised enough that Hart Crane titled the last part (section VIII) of *The Bridge* "Atlantis." Little in the poem has direct bearing on the legendary mid-Atlantic continent mentioned in the *Timaios* and *Critias*. Nor has the poem much to do with Bacon's *The New Atlantis* (though Crane would probably have liked the newness, energy, and utopianism of that work). If the poet used the myth of Atlantis to frame a conclusion for *The Bridge,* only three valences of Atlantis seem to have been adaptable for his purposes: its geographical situation in the Atlantic Ocean, the story of its having sunk beneath the waves when it fell from virtue, and its prophesied resurgence at some future time.

"Thy cables breath the North Atlantic still," a line in the "Proem" has it, and *The Bridge,* among other things, is a poem about the second-largest of the world's oceans. In "Ave Maria," the poem's first section, Columbus crosses the Atlantic, returning eastward to Europe; his destiny is entirely bound up in voyages across that ocean, and the American adventure begins with Columbus's first exploratory crossings. In the poem "Indiana" (which closes section II), the Columbian spirit of adventure has passed into the exploits of the New England whalers of the nineteenth century, represented by a character named Larry, who navigates the sea roads of the Atlantic on his way to Pacific fishing grounds. In the twentieth century, the Atlantic was the first major body of water to be crossed by air—by dirigible and then Lindbergh's solo prop-plane flight in 1927. This event did not leave unmoved the author of "Cape Hatteras." Air travel he saw as an actual, scientific counterpart to the upward spiritual aspiration that was his final subject. During the twenties, all sorts of barriers were being broken. For Crane, the Atlantic serves as a link between America and Europe, between the active present and the contemplative or visionary past. It is not a wall, but a road. A road, but one that keeps all the physical properties and beauty of the liquid state, water in perpetual motion and change.

Like the legendary cities of San Salvador alluded to in "Voyages II," like the Breton cathedral whose legend Debussy enshrined in *La Cathédrale engloutie,* and like Poe's "The City in the Sea," Atlantis was a human dwelling place that perished when the sea overwhelmed it. "The bottom of the sea is cruel," Crane says in "Voyages," but of course he was half in love with it since it stood for one kind of vision— "sleep, death, desire," the poetry of engulfment. Yet the Atlantis of legend was destroyed because its sins offended Neptune, and, insofar as Crane's Atlantis is the *historical* America, he means for this part of the Atlantean symbolic repertory to be active. Long before Crane completed his visionary epic, he was ready to acknowledge that his vision of the New Golden Land and the actual American scene were twain. The United States, however unsinkable, had still fallen below and by far the aspirations of its founders and also below the sanguine estimate propounded by Whitman in *Leaves of Grass.* The historical America appears in *The Bridge* under the sign of fallenness (a prime exception, the paean to air travel in "Cape Hatteras"). So the Atlantis of section VIII is not a historical entity but its visionary counterpart, a new America to which Crane makes or wants to make his voyage. It is the new Atlantis, one resurrected from a watery grave.

Atlantis is "no earthly shore," then, rather the place that answers "the seal's wide spindrift gaze toward paradise." One could as well say, *Paradiso.* For *The Bridge* resembles that other visionary epic by another lyric poet. The journey that

Dante makes, a vast geographical *concetto,* is despite its hundreds of historical referents, essentially a pure vision. Critics used to stress analogies between *Aeneid* and *The Bridge* since Crane mentioned the Latin imperial epic in his letters to Otto Kahn. If Crane's perspective on America had been historical alone, *Aeneid* would in fact be a proper forerunner for Crane's poem. But the *Commedia* is a closer fit and, after all, itself embodies an active relationship to Vergil, to the extent of making Vergil a character in the first two canticles of the poem. For his part, Crane takes the hand of Walt Whitman and lets him be mentor and guide for *The Bridge,* or at least some of its sections. And why not? The only thing near to the nation-founding *Aeneid* in the American tradition is *Leaves of Grass.* In fact, *The Bridge* draws on Vergil, Dante, and Whitman all three, directly or analogically, emphasizing an intertextual relationship that can be found among them already. Crane unquestionably belongs to what might be called the mid-Atlantic tradition in American literature— those writers, like Hawthorne, James, Pound, and Eliot, whose work joins together American and European traditions in order to form something greater than either by itself.

We can establish a few more Dantean connections. First, in both the *Commedia* and *The Bridge* the author appears, however briefly in Crane's poem, as one of the characters, speaking in the first person. (Vergil never does this in *Aeneid.*) The role of Beatrice is parceled out, in *The Bridge,* among several representatives of the Eternal Feminine: the Madre Maria, to whom Columbus prays, and Queen Isabella, under whose auspices he sails; then, Pocahontas, an archetype of incarnation identified with the North American earth, our continent as Indian goddess. Of the poem's two dramatic monologues, one is spoken by the mother figure in "Indiana." Cameo appearances are granted to the "nameless Woman of the South" in "Southern Cross" and then Cathedral Mary of the song "Virginia." Isadora Duncan and Emily Dickinson provide epigraphs for "Quaker Hill" and then are invoked as tutelary spirits in the poem's moving conclusion; they serve as vicarious instances of pain and forbearance. "Atlantis" itself designates no specific female intercessors, mentioning only "sibylline voices," without saying which ones. Perhaps the "Anemone" of Atlantis, the "whitest flower," is meant to be conflated with Dante's paradisal Rose of Light, the circular amphitheater where the saints reign in glory, and where Beatrice, Saint Lucy, and the Blessed Virgin have their seat. There can certainly be no question that, when Crane includes the words "canto" and "canticle" among the lexical profusion of *The Bridge,* he wants to remind us of Dante's epic.

Crane once wrote a short lyric (left unfinished) called "Purgatorio," but *The Bridge* itself is written under two rubrics only, the infernal and the paradisal. They stand next to each other in sequence: Crane has "The Tunnel" lead directly into "Atlantis." It has been remarked that "The Tunnel" is a type of the Orphic or Dantean descent into the underworld. It is also another *Waste Land,* Eliot's own season in *Inferno,* the *paese guasto* that Dante mentions in Canto XIV of the *Commedia's* first canticle. It is not only that *The Waste Land* and *The Bridge* overlap in techniques of allusion and in subject matter: Crane wrote his poem partly in response to Eliot's. *The Bridge,* taken as a whole, becomes a sort of anti–*Waste Land,* by offering an Atlantean or paradisal conclusion to the fallen condition of the modern world as presented in other parts of the poem. (Crane did not live long enough to witness Eliot's own redemption series, *Ash Wednesday* and *The Four Quartets.*) Crane once cried out in a letter to Allen Tate (June 12, 1922): "I have been facing him [Eliot] for *four* years—and while I haven't discovered a weak spot yet in his armour, I flatter myself a little lately that I have discovered a safe tangent to strike which, if I can possibly explain the position,—goes *through* him toward a *different* goal. . . . In his own realm [i.e., Hell] Eliot presents us with an absolute *impasse,* yet oddly enough, he can be utilized to lead us to, intelligently point to, other positions and 'pastures new.'"

The tag from the last line of *Lycidas,* recalling sunrise on "fresh woods and Pastures new," needs to be placed beside another from Blake's "Morning," which is used as an epigraph for "The Tunnel."

> To find the Western path
> Right thro' the Gates of Wrath.

We must keep in mind that *Lycidas* is an elegy for a young man drowned on a sea voyage; that section IV of *The Waste Land,* "Death by Water," recounts the death at sea of a young, handsome sailor; that "The Tunnel" is clearly modeled on Eliot, with Eliot's precursor Poe present as a character in the poem, and that "The Tunnel" embodies a subway ride under the East River to Brooklyn as a prelude to the last section of the poem. In Blake's "Morning," one travels east to reach a "Land of Pity" in the West. This journey reverses Columbus's navigational paradox of traveling west to reach the East, but we recall that in "Ave Maria," it is an eastward trajectory that Crane gives Columbus. Crane's interborough subway ride takes the same general direction, beginning near *Columbus* Circle, then pushing downtown and eastward under the city and harbor to reach *Columbia* Heights, with its prospect on the Brooklyn Bridge. This mundane transit completes the eastward thrust begun in "Indiana," where (as the monologue tells us) a pioneer family has come home, after a failed fling at the Colorado gold rush, to a farm in the Midwest; the son Larry will continue on to the Atlantic seaboard and sign on as a whaler. If there is a moral here, it touches on the question of greed and the redemption from it. In order for America to achieve spiritual regeneration, it must go east and begin to seek deeper sanctions for life than have been operative before. *

---

*The West-East directional paradox also figures in another poem that Crane, the disciple of Donne, would certainly have known. That is

From "The Tunnel," with its nightmare vision of commercialism and human debasement, the reader is led to a new prospect at ground level, a westward vista toward the Bridge—but not the Brooklyn Bridge merely. This time it is, by poetic alchemy, "Atlantis." Gazing at the Atlantis Bridge, perhaps we will be able to focus on something difficult to see because it is too obvious: the Bridge goes in two directions, east and west. To link is to comprise a relation in two directions. Crane wants to stress that truth not just for space but for time as well. In strophe four he speaks of

> towering looms that press
> Sidelong with flight of blade on tendon blade
> —Tomorrows into yesteryear—and link
> What cipher-script of time no traveller reads
> But who, through smoking pyres of love and death
> Searches the timeless laugh of mythic spears.

"Spears" is a pun for "spheres," and, in the visionary sphere, time may run back as well as forward, as the phrase "Tomorrows into yesteryear" implies. Linkage, even for time, is mutual-reciprocal. America's future *in Atlantis* can

---

Donne's "Goodfriday, 1613. Riding Westward," which opens with these lines:

> Let mans Soule be a Spheare, and then, in this,
> The intelligence that moves, devotion is,
> And as the other Spheares, by being grown
> Subject to forraigne motions, lose their owne,
> And being by others hurried every day,
> Scarce in a yeare their naturall forme obey:
> Pleasure or businesse, so, our Soules admit
> For their first mover, and are whirled by it.
> Hence is't, that I am carryed towards the West
> This day, when my Soules forme bends toward the East.
> There I should see a Sunne, by rising set,
> And by that setting endlesse day beget;
> But that Christ on this Crosse, did rise and fall,
> Sinne had eternally benighted all.

move through the present back as far as it can discover relation—to Whitman, to fourteenth-century Italy, or even Homer's Hellas and the Bible.

Of course Whitman's example is the most immediate and compelling. In his "Crossing Brooklyn Ferry" he raises a celebratory shout, "It avails not, time nor place—distance avails not." This is not a statement compatible with history, but "Atlantis" can accommodate it, rising to a realm freed from the constraints of chronology, geography, and finally of logic. Atlantis's ascension is already foreshadowed by one of the ship names in "Cutty Sark": *"ATLANTIS ROSE drums wreathe the rose, / the star floats burning in a gulf of tears / and sleep another thousand—."* The sentence doesn't parse readily, but in it we can see the millenary hope of resurgence, an event signaled at the verbal level by the homonymic pun formed by the past tense of *rise* and the visionary, paradisal flower. In "Atlantis" the rose is recast as the anemone, or windflower, whose name is derived from Greek, *anemos* for "wind," similar to the Latin *anima*, or "soul." For the Atlantean ascension to take place, visionary power of the soul is required. That is what Whitman's celebratory shout is meant to stir up in the reader, and Crane intends to answer it.

Crane had already made a trial run of *The Bridge*'s visionary ascending trajectory in "Voyages." The fundamental psychological and metaphysical drama is the same in both poems, but with different referential objects. "Voyages" traces the contour of a love and its poetic expression, moving from joint ecstasy to a kind of drowning, the death of that love, and finally a substitution (or fulfillment) of it in a larger-than-personal vision. The sequence moves from the "incarnate word" of IV to the "imaged Word" of VI. So with *The Bridge*. In this case, however, the loved object is America, the historical America epitomized by the Brooklyn Bridge. But this America is compromised by historical failure, as Crane shows us in "Quaker Hill" and in the submerging "The Tunnel." The poet must summon a new immaterial vehicle for his aspirations, and what rises from baptismal waters in section VIII is the Atlantis Bridge.

We have seen how Crane used the East-West axis as a structural component of his poem, but there is another axis equally important. The "Atlantis" Bridge goes in two directions spatially and temporally, but the most frequently invoked directional cue in the poem is an upward vector. It makes us conscious that the down-up axis has also been at work in the architecture of *The Bridge,* most noticeably in "The Tunnel," where the downward vector was pursued to its lowest spatial and spiritual point. These coordinate axes, East-West and down-up, embody a thematic suggestion present in the epigraph used for the whole of *The Bridge.* It comes from the first chapter of Job: "From going to and fro in the earth, and walking up and down in it." Crane, a visionary in the hopeful mode, concludes his epic with the upward-soaring section VIII, one of the few examples of the high Romantic Sublime written in this ironic and reductive century.

The new Atlantis is not America, and yet it still might be. Or rather America is Atlantis insofar as it is *going* to be Atlantis, insofar as it is the land where "connecting" is a central spiritual activity. In an essay called "The Spiritual Problem of Modern Man" published in 1928, Jung says "today has meaning only if it stands between yesterday and tomorrow. It is a process of transition that forms the link between past and future. Only the man who is conscious of the present in this sense may call himself modern." Crane was a poet of the "years of the modern" in exactly this sense. And he considered America as the most likely theater, among nations of the world, for linkage of this kind. In the Brooklyn Bridge Crane saw a striking visual realization of this theme. The bridge was a marvel of modern engineering, lightweight catenary suspension arranged in a beautiful harplike form, the suspension webbing anchored to two stone piers comprising twin Gothic ogival arches. It is a wedding of the Gothic with the modern, and the same fusion can be seen in the Woolworth Building, which is the haunt of Cathedral Mary in the poem "Virginia" from section V. (In its day the Woolworth was known as the Cathedral of Commerce.) These two examples of architectural futurism, already venerably obsolete when Crane turned to them, were to be taken as models of the spiritual connectivity the poet considered the most valid kind of artistic modernism.

America will be Crane's Atlantis whenever Americans see themselves as "a bridge to their better selves," as Nietzsche puts it. Whenever love is a connection mutually realized. Whenever a new American poem looks backward to great precursors to make a comradely handclasp across the centuries. Whenever acts of the imagination look *forward* to other later consciousnesses who will receive them. (It is in this sense that Crane means, "O Thou whose radiance doth inherit me," a statement presupposing radiant acts of receptivity on the part of those who come after. No other use of the first-person pronoun occurs in "Atlantis.") Atlantis is present, finally, whenever earthly vistas lead through covenantal paths upward toward the ideal and divine, so that the Brooklyn Bridge becomes the Atlantis Bridge, is both Cathay and the Psalm of Cathay.

The most frequent trope in section VIII is simple metaphoric equation, *B* equals *A,* and so forth. The bridge is apostrophized in more than a dozen different ways, nor is there any effort to harmonize the widely varying epithets. What single entity could be all of the following? Brooklyn Bridge; America; Cathay; Atlantis; Paradiso; the Psalm of Cathay; Vision-of-the-Voyage; Choir; "white pervasive Paradigm" of love, "steeled Cognizance"; "intrinsic Myth"; "Deity's glittering pledge"; "whitest flower, Answerer . . . Anemone"; "One Song, one Bridge of Fire." If this logically meaningless entity is given Crane's title—"Atlantis"—and its central function of "connecting" kept in mind, we can see that the Atlantean rhetorical figure, above all others, is metaphor. The Greek root of the word, *metaphórein,* suggests a "bearing across," "transport beyond." The accumulation of metaphoric terms in "Atlantis," carried beyond the bounds of literary decorum, is really a ritual enactment in homage to the figure of metaphor and the psychic processes that go with it.

As vision is a metaphor for poetry, and poetry, a metaphor for its subject, in the largest perspective all things can be metaphors for all others, and reciprocally, a tenet central to mystic philosophies of many varieties. The "incarnate word" is a metaphor for the "imaged Word," and reciprocally. God is a metaphor for each human being, and reciprocally. I am a metaphor for Thou, and reciprocally. Through visionary metaphor, through "transport," we can be the Bridge, or "connecting." And, if we are, Atlantis rises up again beneath our bootsoles, so that the answer to the question asked in the last lines of "Atlantis"—"Is it Cathay?"—may always be for any one of a series of answerers, yes.